Richard Lovell Edgeworth

Richard Lovell Edgeworth

A selection from his memoirs

Richard Lovell Edgeworth

Richard Lovell Edgeworth
A selection from his memoirs

ISBN/EAN: 9783337276324

Printed in Europe, USA, Canada, Australia, Japan

Cover: Foto ©Raphael Reischuk / pixelio.de

More available books at **www.hansebooks.com**

Richard Lovell Edgeworth

A SELECTION FROM HIS MEMOIRS

EDITED BY

BEATRIX L. TOLLEMACHE

(HON. MRS. LIONEL TOLLEMACHE)

RIVINGTON, PERCIVAL & CO.

KING STREET, COVENT GARDEN

LONDON

1896

LIFE IS AN INN

THERE is an inn where many a guest
May enter, tarry, take his rest.
When he departs there's nought to pay,
Only he carries nought away.

'Not so,' I cried, 'for raiment fine,
Sweet thoughts, heart-joys, and hopes that shine,
May clothe anew his flitting form,
As wings that change the creeping worm.
His toil-worn garb he casts aside,
And journeys onward glorified.'

B. L. T.

RICHARD LOVELL EDGEWORTH

CHAPTER I

SOME years ago, I came across the *Memoirs of Richard Lovell Edgeworth* in a second-hand book-shop, and found it so full of interest and amusement, that I am tempted to draw the attention of other readers to it. As the volumes are out of print, I have not hesitated to make long extracts from them. The first volume is autobiographical, and the narrative is continued in the second volume by Edgeworth's daughter Maria, who was her father's constant companion, and was well fitted to carry out his wish that she should complete the *Memoirs*.

Richard Lovell Edgeworth was born at Bath in 1744. He was a shining example of what a good landlord can do for his tenants, and how an active mind will always find objects of interest without constantly requiring what are called amusements; for the leisure class should be like Sundays in a week, and as the ideal Sunday should be a day when we

A

can store up good and beautiful thoughts to refresh us during the week, a day when there is no hurry, no urgent business to trouble us, a day when we have time to rise above the sordid details of life and enjoy its beauties; so it seems to me that those who are not obliged to work for their living should do their part in the world by adding to its store of good and wise thoughts, by cultivating the arts and raising the standard of excellence in them, and by bringing to light truths which had been forgotten, or which had been hidden from our forefathers.

Richard Edgeworth was eminently a practical man, impulsive, as we learn from his imprudent marriage at nineteen, but with a strong sense of duty. His mother, who was Welsh, brought him up in habits of thrift and industry very unlike those of his ancestors, which he records in the early pages of his *Memoirs*. His great-grandmother seems to have been a woman of strong character and courage in spite of her belief in fairies and her dread of them, for he writes that 'while she was living at Liscard, she was, on some sudden alarm, obliged to go at night to a garret at the top of the house for some gunpowder, which was kept there in a barrel. She was followed upstairs by an ignorant servant girl, who carried a bit of candle without a candlestick between her fingers. When Lady Edgeworth had taken what gunpowder she wanted, had locked the door, and was halfway downstairs again, she observed that the girl had not her candle, and asked what she had done with it; the girl recollected, and answered that she had left it *"stuck in the barrel of black salt."* Lady Edgeworth bid her stand still, and instantly returned by herself to the room where the gunpowder was, found the candle as the girl had described, put her hand carefully underneath it, carried it safely out, and when she got to the bottom of the stairs dropped on her knees, and thanked God for their deliverance.'

When we remember that it was Richard Edgeworth, the father of Maria, who trained and encouraged her first efforts in literature, we feel that we owe him a debt of gratitude ; but our interest is increased when we read his *Memoirs*, for we then find ourselves brought into close contact with a very intelligent and vigorous mind, keen to take part in the scientific experiments of the day, while his upright moral character and earnest and well-directed efforts to improve his Irish property win our admiration ; and when we remember that he married in succession four wives, and preserved harmony among the numerous members of his household, our admiration becomes wonder, and we would fain learn the secret of his success. One element in his success doubtless

was that he kept every one around him usefully
employed, and in the manner most suited to each.
He knew how to develop innate talent, and did not
crush or overpower those around him. He owed
much to the early training of a sensible mother, and
he gives an anecdote of his early childhood, which I
will quote :—

'My mother was not blind to my faults. She saw
the danger of my passionate temper. It was a difficult task to correct it ; though perfectly submissive
to her, I was with others rebellious and outrageous
in my anger. My mother heard continual complaints
of me; yet she wisely forbore to lecture or punish me
for every trifling misdemeanour ; she seized proper
occasions to make a strong impression upon my
mind.

'One day my elder brother Tom, who, as I have
said, was almost a man when I was a little child,
came into the nursery where I was playing, and
where the maids were ironing. Upon some slight
provocation or contradiction from him, I flew into a
violent passion ; and, snatching up one of the box-
irons which the maid had just laid down, I flung it
across the table at my brother. He stooped instantly;
and, thank God! it missed him. There was a red-
hot heater in it, of which I knew nothing until I saw
it thrown out, and until I heard the scream from the

maids. They seized me, and dragged me downstairs to my mother. Knowing that she was extremely fond of my brother, and that she was of a warm indignant temper, they expected that signal vengeance would burst upon me. They all spoke at once. When my mother heard what I had done, I saw she was struck with horror, but she said not one word in anger to me. She ordered everybody out of the room except myself, and then drawing me near her, she spoke to me in a mild voice, but in a most serious manner. First, she explained to me the nature of the crime which I had run the hazard of committing; she told me she was sure that I had no intention seriously to hurt my brother, and did not know that if the iron had hit my brother, it must have killed him. While I felt this first shock, and whilst the horror of murder was upon me, my mother seized the moment to conjure me to try in future to command my passions. I remember her telling me that I had an uncle by the mother's side who had such a violent temper, that in a fit of passion one of his eyes actually started out of its socket. "You," said my mother to me, "have naturally a violent temper; if you grow up to be a man without learning to govern it, it will be impossible for you then to command yourself; and there is no knowing what crime you may in a fit of passion commit, and how miserable you may, in consequence of it, become. You are but a very young child, yet I think you can understand me. Instead of speaking to you as I do at this moment, I might punish you severely; but I think it better to treat you like a reasonable creature. My wish is to teach you to command your temper; nobody can do that for you so well as you can do it for yourself."

' As nearly as I can recollect, these were my mother's words; I am certain this was the sense of what she then said to me. The impression made by the earnest solemnity with which she spoke never, during the whole course of my life, was effaced from my mind. From that moment I determined to govern my temper.'

Acting upon the old adage that example is better than precept, his mother taught him at an early age to observe the good and bad qualities of the persons he met. The study of character she justly felt to be most important, and yet it is not one of the subjects taught in schools except by personal collision with other boys, and incidentally in reading history. When sent to school at Warwick, he learned not only the first rudiments of grammar, but 'also the rudiments of that knowledge which leads us to observe the difference of tempers and characters in our fellow-creatures. The marking how widely they differ, and by what minute varieties they are

distinguished, continues, to the end of life, an in-
exhaustible subject of discrimination ! '

May not Maria have gained much valuable
training in the art of novel-writing from a father
who was so impressed with the value of the study of
character ?

The Gospel precept which we read as 'Judge not,'
should surely be translated 'Condemn not,' and does
not forbid a mental exercise which is necessary in our
intercourse with others.

Among the circumstances which had considerable
influence on his character, he mentions : ' My mother
was reading to me some passages from Shakespeare's
plays, marking the characters of Coriolanus and of
Julius Cæsar, which she admired. The contempt
which Coriolanus expresses for the opinion and
applause of the vulgar, for "the voices of the greasy-
headed multitude," suited well with that disdain for
low company with which I had been first inspired by
the fable of the Lion and the Cub.[1]   It is probable
that I understood the speeches of Coriolanus but
imperfectly ; yet I know that I sympathised with my
mother's admiration, my young spirit was touched by
his noble character, by his generosity, and, above all,
by his filial piety and his gratitude to his mother.'
He mentions also that 'some traits in the history of

[1] In Gay's *Fables.*

Cyrus, which was read to me, seized my imagination,
and, next to Joseph in the Old Testament, Cyrus
became the favourite of my childhood. My sister
and I used to amuse ourselves with playing Cyrus
at the court of his grandfather Astyages. At the
great Persian feasts, I was, like young Cyrus, to set
an example of temperance, to eat nothing but water-
cresses, to drink nothing but water, and to reprove
the cupbearer for making the king, my grandfather,
drunk. To this day I remember the taste of those
water-cresses ; and for those who love to trace the
characters of men in the sports of children, I may
mention that my character for sobriety, if not for
water-drinking, has continued through life.'

When Richard Edgeworth encouraged his daughter
Maria's literary tastes, he was doubtless mindful how
much pleasure and support his own mother had
derived from studying the best authors ; and when we
read later of the affectionate terms on which Maria
stood with her various stepmothers and their families,
we cannot help thinking that she must have inherited
at least one of the beautiful traits in her grandmother's
character which Richard Edgeworth especially dwells
on : ' She had the most generous disposition that I ever
met with ; not only that common generosity, which
parts with money, or money's worth, freely, and
almost without the right hand knowing what the left

hand doeth ; but she had also an entire absence of
selfish consideration. Her own wishes or opinions
were never pursued merely because they were her
own ; the ease and comfort of everybody about her
were necessary for her well-being. Every distress,
as far as her fortune, or her knowledge, or her wit
or eloquence could reach, was alleviated or removed ;
and, above all, she could forgive, and sometimes even
forget injuries.'

Richard's taste for science early showed itself,
when at seven years old his curiosity was excited
by an electric battery which was applied to his
mother's paralysed side. He says :—

'At this time electricity was but little known in
Ireland, and its fame as a cure for palsy had been
considerably magnified. It, as usual, excited some
sensation in the paralytic limbs on the first trials.
One of the experiments on my mother failed of
producing a shock, and Mr. Deane seemed at a loss
to account for it. I had observed that the wire
which was used to conduct the electric fluid, had,
as it hung in a curve from the instrument to my
mother's arm, touched the hinge of a table which
was in the way, and I had the courage to mention
this circumstance, which was the real cause of
failure.'

It was when he was eight years old, and while

travelling with his father, that his attention was caught by 'a man carrying a machine five or six feet in diameter, of an oval form, and composed of slender ribs of steel. I begged my father to inquire what it was. We were told that it was the skeleton of a lady's hoop. It was furnished with hinges, which permitted it to fold together in a small compass, so that more than two persons might sit on one seat of a coach—a feat not easily performed, when ladies were encompassed with whalebone hoops of six feet extent. My curiosity was excited by the first sight of this machine, probably more than another child's might have been, because previous agreeable associations had given me some taste for mechanics, which was still a little further increased by the pleasure I took in examining this glittering contrivance. Thus even the most trivial incidents in childhood act reciprocally as cause and effect in forming our tastes.'

It was in 1754 that Mrs. Edgeworth, continuing much out of health, resolved to consult a certain Lord Trimblestone, who had been very successful in curing various complaints. Lord Trimblestone received Mr. and Mrs. Edgeworth most cordially and hospitably, and though he could not hope to cure her, recommended some palliatives. He had more success with another lady whose disorder was purely nervous. His treatment of her was so original that I must quote it at length :—

'Instead of a grave and forbidding physician, her host, she found, was a man of most agreeable manners. Lady Trimblestone did everything in her power to entertain her guest, and for two or three days the demon of *ennui* was banished. At length the lady's vapours returned ; everything appeared changed. Melancholy brought on a return of alarming nervous complaints—convulsions of the limbs—perversion of the understanding—a horror of society ; in short, all the complaints that are to be met with in an advertisement enumerating the miseries of a nervous patient. In the midst of one of her most violent fits, four mutes, dressed in white, entered her apartment ; slowly approaching her, they took her without violence in their arms, and without giving her time to recollect herself, conveyed her into a distant chamber hung with black and lighted with green tapers. From the ceiling, which was of a considerable height, a swing was suspended, in which she was placed by the mutes, so as to be seated at some distance from the ground. One of the mutes set the swing in motion ; and as it approached one end of the room, she was opposed by a grim menacing figure armed with a huge rod of birch. When she looked behind her, she saw a similar figure at

the other end of the room, armed in the same
manner.   The terror, notwithstanding the strange
circumstances which surrounded her, was not of
that sort which threatens life ; but every instant
there was an immediate hazard of bodily pain.
After some time, the mutes appeared again, with
great composure took the lady out of the swing,
and conducted her to her apartment.   When she
had reposed some time, a servant came to inform
her that tea was ready.   Fear of what might be
the consequence of a refusal prevented her from
declining to appear.   No notice was taken of what
had happened, and the evening and the next day
passed without any attack of her disorder.   On the
third day the vapours returned—the mutes reappeared
—the menacing flagellants again affrighted her, and
again she enjoyed a remission of her complaints.
By degrees the fits of her disorder became less frequent, the ministration of her tormentors less necessary, and in time the habits of hypochondriacism
were so often interrupted, and such a new series of
ideas was introduced into her mind, that she recovered perfect health, and preserved to the end of
her life sincere gratitude for her adventurous physician.'

Three years were spent by Richard at Corpus
Christi College, Oxford, while his vacations were

often passed at Bath by the wish of his father, who
was anxious that his son should be introduced to good
society at an early age. It was there that Richard
saw Beau Nash, 'the popular monarch of Bath,' and
also 'the remains of the celebrated Lord Chesterfield.
I looked in vain for that fire, which we expect to
see in the eye of a man of wit and genius. He
was obviously unhappy, and a melancholy spectacle.'

Of the young ladies he says: 'I soon perceived
that those who made the best figure in the ballroom
were not always qualified to please in conversation ;
I saw that beauty and grace were sometimes accompanied by a frivolous character, by disgusting envy,
or despicable vanity. All this I had read of in poetry
and prose ; but there is a wide difference, especially
among young people, between what is read and
related, and what is actually seen. Books and advice
make much more impression in proportion as we
grow older. We find by degrees that those who
lived before us have recorded as the result of their
experience the very things that we observe to be
true.'

It was while still at college that he married Miss
Elers without waiting for his father's consent ; he
soon found that his young wife did not sympathise
with his pursuits ; but he adds, 'Though I heartily
repented my folly, I determined to bear with firmness

and temper the evil, which I had brought upon myself. Perhaps pride had some share in my resolution.'

He had a son before he was twenty, and soon afterwards took his wife to Edgeworth Town to introduce her to his parents; but a few days after his arrival his mother, who had long been an invalid, felt that her end was approaching, and calling him to her bedside, told him, with a sort of pleasure, that she felt she should die before night. She added: 'If there is a state of just retribution in another world, I must be happy, for I have suffered during the greatest part of my life, and I know that I did not deserve it by my thoughts or actions.'

Her dying advice to him was, '"My son, learn how to say No." She warned me further of an error into which, from the vivacity of my temper, I was most likely to fall. "Your inventive faculty," said she, "will lead you eagerly into new plans; and you may be dazzled by some new scheme before you have finished, or fairly tried what you had begun. Resolve to finish; never procrastinate." '

IT was in 1765, while stopping at Chester and examining a mechanical exhibition there, that Edgeworth first heard of Dr. Darwin, who had lately invented a carriage which could turn in a small compass without danger of upsetting. Richard on hearing this determined to try his hand on coach building, and had a handsome phaeton constructed upon the same principle; this he showed in London to the Society for the Encouragement of Arts, and mentioned that he owed the original idea to Dr. Darwin. He then wrote to the latter describing the reception of his invention, and was invited to his house. The doctor was out when he arrived at Lichfield, but Mrs. Darwin received him, and after some conversation on books and prints asked him to drink tea. He discovered later that Dr. Darwin had imagined him to be a coachmaker, but that Mrs. Darwin had found out the mistake. 'When supper was nearly finished, a loud rapping at the door announced the doctor. There was a bustle

in the hall, which made Mrs. Darwin get up and go
to the door. Upon her exclaiming that they were
bringing in a dead man, I went to the hall: I saw
some persons, directed by one whom I guessed to be
Dr. Darwin, carrying a man, who appeared motion-
less. "He is not dead," said Dr. Darwin. "He
is only dead drunk. I found him," continued the
doctor, "nearly suffocated in a ditch; I had him
lifted into my carriage, and brought hither, that
we might take care of him to-night." Candles came,
and what was the surprise of the doctor and of Mrs.
Darwin to find that the person whom he had saved
was Mrs. Darwin's brother! who, for the first time
in his life, as I was assured, had been intoxicated
in this manner, and who would undoubtedly have
perished had it not been for Dr. Darwin's humanity.

'During this scene I had time to survey my new
friend, Dr. Darwin. He was a large man, fat, and
rather clumsy; but intelligence and benevolence were
painted in his countenance. He had a considerable
impediment in his speech, a defect which is in general
painful to others; but the doctor repaid his auditors
so well for making them wait for his wit or his knowledge, that he seldom found them impatient.'

At Lichfield he met Mr. Bolton of Snow Hill, Birmingham, who asked him to his house, and showed
him over the principal manufactories of Birmingham,

where he further improved his knowledge of practical mechanics. His time was now principally devoted to inventions ; he received a silver medal in 1768 from the Society of Arts for a *perambulator*, as he calls it, an instrument for measuring land. This is a curious instance of the changed use of a word, as we now associate *perambulators* with babies. In 1769 he received the Society's gold medal for various machines, and about this time produced what might have been the forerunner of the bicycle, 'a huge hollow wheel made very light, withinside of which, in a barrel of six feet diameter, a man should walk. Whilst he stepped thirty inches, the circumference of the large wheel, or rather wheels, would revolve five feet on the ground ; and as the machine was to roll on planks, and on a plane somewhat inclined, when once the *vis inertiæ* of the machine should be over-come, it would carry on the man within it as fast as he could possibly walk. . . . It was not finished ; I had not yet furnished it with the means of stopping or moderating its motion. A young lad got into it, his companions launched it on a path which led gently down hill towards a very steep chalk-pit. This pit was at such a distance as to be out of their thoughts when they set the wheel in motion. On it ran. The lad withinside plied his legs with all his might. The spectators who at first stood still to

behold the operation were soon alarmed by the shouts
of their companion, who perceived his danger. The
vehicle became quite ungovernable; the velocity increased as it ran down hill. Fortunately, the boy
contrived to jump from his rolling prison before it
reached the chalk-pit; but the wheel went on with
such velocity as to outstrip its pursuers, and, rolling
over the edge of the precipice, it was dashed to
pieces.

'The next day, when I came to look for my machine,
intending to try it upon some planks, which had been
laid for it, I found, to my no small disappointment,
that the object of all my labours and my hopes was
lying at the bottom of a chalk-pit, broken into a
thousand pieces. I could not at that time afford to
construct another wheel of that sort, and I cannot
therefore determine what might have been the success
of my scheme.'

He goes on to say: 'I shall mention a sailing
carriage that I tried on this common. The carriage
was light, steady, and ran with amazing velocity.
One day, when I was preparing for a sail in it with
my friend and schoolfellow, Mr. William Foster, my
wheel-boat escaped from its moorings just as we were
going to step on board. With the utmost difficulty I
overtook it; and as I saw three or four stage-coaches
on the road, and feared that this sailing chariot might

frighten their horses, I, at the hazard of my life, got
into my carriage while it was under full sail, and then,
at a favourable part of the road, I used the means I
had of guiding it easily out of the way. But the
sense of the mischief which must have ensued if I
had not succeeded in getting into the machine at the
proper place, and stopping it at the right moment,
was so strong, as to deter me from trying any more experiments on this carriage in such a dangerous place.'

I have already given the changed use of the word
perambulator. As an example of the different use of
a word in the last century, I may mention telegraph,
by which he means signalling either by moving
wooden arms or by showing lights. This mode of
conveying a message he first applied in order to win
a wager : 'A famous match was at that time pending
at Newmarket between two horses that were in every
respect as nearly equal as possible. Lord March, one
evening at Ranelagh, expressed his regret to Sir
Francis Delaval that he was not able to attend Newmarket at the next meeting. " I am obliged," said he,
" to stay in London ; I shall, however, be at the Turf
Coffee-house ; I shall station fleet horses on the road
to bring me the earliest intelligence of the event of
the race, and I shall manage my bets accordingly."

' I asked at what time in the evening he expected to
know who was winner. He said about nine in the

evening. I asserted that I should be able to name the winning horse at four o'clock in the afternoon. Lord March heard my assertion with so much incredulity, as to urge me to defend myself; and at length I offered to lay five hundred pounds that I would in London name the winning horse at Newmarket at five o'clock in the evening of the day when the great match in question was to be run.'

The wager was however given up when Edgeworth told Lord March that he did not depend upon the fleetness or strength of horses to carry the desired intelligence.

His friend, Sir Francis Delaval, immediately put up under his directions an apparatus between his house and part of Piccadilly. He adds: 'I also set up a night telegraph between a house which Sir Francis Delaval occupied at Hampstead, and one to which I had access in Great Russell Street, Bloomsbury. This nocturnal telegraph answered well, but was too expensive for common use.' Later on he writes to Dr. Darwin :—

'I have been employed for two months in experiments upon a telegraph of my own invention. By day, at eighteen or twenty miles distance, I show, by four pointers, isosceles triangles, twenty feet high, on four imaginary circles, eight imaginary points, which correspond with the figures 0, 1, 2, 3, 4, 5, 6, 7, so that seven thousand different combinations are formed, of four figures each, which refer to a dictionary of words. By night, white lights are used.'

Dr. Darwin in reply says: 'The telegraph you described, I dare say, would answer the purpose. It would be like a giant wielding his long arms and talking with his fingers: and those long arms might be covered with lamps in the night.'

It is curious now to read Mr. Edgeworth's words: 'I will venture to predict that it will at some future period be generally practised, not only in these islands, but that it will in time become a means of communication between the most distant parts of the world, wherever arts and sciences have civilised mankind.'

It was some years later, in 1794, when Ireland was in a disturbed state, and threatened by a French invasion, that Edgeworth laid his scheme for telegraphs before the Government, and offered to keep open communication between Dublin and Cork if the Government would pay the expense. He made a trial between two hills fifteen miles apart, and a message was sent and an answer received in five minutes. The Government paid little attention to his offer, and finally refused it. Two months later the French were on the Irish coasts, and great confusion and distress was occasioned by the want of accurate news. 'The troops were harassed with contradictory orders and forced marches for want of intelligence, and from that indecision, which must always be the consequence of insufficient information. Many days were spent in terror, and in fruitless wishes for an English fleet. . . . At last Ireland was providentially saved by the change of the wind, which prevented the enemy from effecting a landing on her coast.'

Another of Edgeworth's inventions was a one-wheeled carriage adapted to go over narrow roads ; it was made fast by shafts to the horse's sides, and was furnished with two weights or counterpoises that hung below the shafts. In this carriage he travelled to Birmingham and astonished the country folk on the way.

I must now give a sketch of Edgeworth's matrimonial adventures. They began after a strange fashion, when, at fifteen, he and some young companions had a merry-making at his sister's marriage, and one of the party putting on a white cloak as a surplice, proposed to marry Richard to a young lady who was his favourite partner. With the door key as a ring the mock parson gabbled over a few words of the marriage service. When Richard's father heard of this mock marriage he was so alarmed that he treated it seriously, and sued and got a divorce for his son in the ecclesiastical court.

It was while visiting Dr. Darwin at Lichfield that Edgeworth made some friendships which influenced his whole life. At the Bishop's Palace, where Canon Seward lived, he first met Miss Honora Sneyd, who was brought up as a daughter by Mrs. Seward. He was much struck by her beauty and by her mental gifts, and says : 'Now for the first time in my life, I saw a woman that equalled the picture of perfection which existed in my imagination. I had long suffered much from the want of that cheerfulness in a wife, without which marriage could not be agreeable to a man with such a temper as mine. I had borne this evil, I believe, with patience ; but my not being happy at home exposed me to the danger of being too happy elsewhere.' He describes in another place his first wife as 'prudent, domestic, and affectionate ; but she was not of a cheerful temper. She lamented about trifles ; and the lamenting of a female with whom we live does not render home delightful.'

His friend, Mr. Day,[1] was also intimate at the Palace, but did not admire Honora at that time (1770) as much as Edgeworth did. Mr. Day thought 'she danced too well ; she had too much an air of fashion in her dress and manners ; and her arms were not sufficiently round and white to please him.'

He was at this time much preoccupied with an

---

[1] The author of *Sandford and Merton.*

orphan, Sabrina Sydney, whom he had taken from the Foundling Hospital, and whom he was educating with the idea of marrying her ultimately. Honora, on the other hand, had received the addresses of Mr. André, afterwards Major André, who was shot as a spy during the American War. But want of fortune caused the parents on both sides to discourage this attachment, and it was broken off.

It was in 1771 that Mr. Day, having placed Sabrina at a boarding-school, became conscious of Honora's attractions, and began to think of marrying her. 'He wrote me one of the most eloquent letters I ever read,' says Edgeworth, 'to point out to me the folly and meanness of indulging a hopeless passion for any woman, let her merit be what it might; declaring at the same time that he "never would marry so as to divide himself from his chosen friend. Tell me," said he, "have you sufficient strength of mind totally to subdue love that cannot be indulged with peace, or honour, or virtue?"

'I answered that nothing but trial could make me acquainted with the influence which reason might have over my feelings; that I would go with my family to Lichfield, where I could be in the company of the dangerous object; and that I would faithfully acquaint him with all my thoughts and feelings. We went to Lichfield, and stayed there for some time with Mr. Day. I saw him continually in company with Honora Sneyd. I saw that he was received with approbation, and that he looked forward to marrying her at no very distant period. When I saw this, I can affirm with truth that I felt pleasure, and even exultation. I looked to the happiness of two people for whom I had the most perfect esteem, without the intervention of a single sentiment or feeling that could make me suspect I should ever repent having been instrumental to their union.'

Later on Mr. Day wrote a long letter to Honora, describing his scheme of life (which was very peculiar), and his admiration for her, and asking whether she could return his affections and be willing to lead the secluded life which was his ideal. This letter he gave to Edgeworth to deliver. 'I took the packet; my friend requested that I would go to the Palace and deliver it myself. I went, and I delivered it with real satisfaction to Honora. She desired me to come next morning for an answer. . . . I gave the answer to Mr. Day, and left him to peruse it by himself. When I returned, I found him actually in a fever. The letter contained an excellent answer to his arguments in favour of the rights of men, and a clear, dispassionate view of the rights of women.

'Miss Honora Sneyd would not admit the unqualified control of a husband over all her actions.

She did not feel that seclusion from society was
indispensably necessary to preserve female virtue,
or to secure domestic happiness.   Upon terms of
reasonable equality she supposed that mutual confidence might best subsist.   She said that, as Mr.
Day had decidedly declared his determination to live
in perfect seclusion from what is usually called the
world, it was fit she should decidedly declare that
she would not change her present mode of life, with
which she had no reason to be dissatisfied, for any
dark and untried system that could be proposed to
her. . . . One restraint, which had acted long and
steadily upon my feelings, was now removed; my
friend was no longer attached to Miss Honora Sneyd.
My former admiration of her returned with unabated
ardour. . . . This admiration was unknown to everybody but Mr. Day ; . . . he represented to me the
danger, the criminality of such an attachment; I
knew that there is but one certain method of
escaping such dangers—*flight.*   I resolved to go
abroad.'

MR. DAY and Edgeworth went to France, and the latter spent nearly two years at Lyons, where his wife joined him. Here he found interest and occupation in some engineering works by which the course of the Rhone was to be diverted and some land gained to enlarge the city, which lies hemmed in between the Rhone and the Saone. When the works were nearly completed, an old boatman warned Edgeworth 'that a tremendous flood might be expected in ten days from the mountains of Savoy. I represented this to the company, and proposed to employ more men, and to engage, by increased wages, those who were already at work, to continue every day till it was dark ; but I could not persuade them to a sudden increase of their expenditure. . . . At five or six o'clock one morning, I was awakened by a prodigious noise on the ramparts under my windows. I sprang out of bed, and saw numbers of people rushing towards the Rhone. I foreboded the disaster ! dressed myself, and hastened to the river. . . . When I reached the Rhone, I beheld a tremendous sight! All the work of several weeks, carried on daily by nearly a hundred men, had been swept away. Piles, timber, barrows, tools, and large parts of expensive machinery were all carried down the torrent, and thrown in broken pieces upon the banks. The principal part of the machinery had been erected upon an island opposite the rampart; here there still remained some valuable timber and engines, which might, probably, be saved by immediate exertion. The old boatman, whom I have mentioned before, was at the water-side; I asked him to row me over to the island, that I might give orders how to preserve what remained belonging to the company. My old friend, the boatman, represented to me, with great kindness, the imminent danger to which I should expose myself. " Sir," he added, "the best swimmer in Lyons, unless he were one of the *Rhone-men*, could not save himself if the boat overset, and you cannot swim at all."

' " Very true," I replied, " but the boat will not overset ; and both my duty and my honour require that I should run every hazard for those who have put so much trust in me." My old boatman took me over safely, and left me on the island ; but in returning by himself, the poor fellow's little boat was caught by a wave, and it skimmed to the bottom like a slate or an oyster-shell that is thrown obliquely into the water. A general exclamation was uttered from the shore; but, in a few minutes, the boatman was seen sitting upon a row of piles in the middle of the river, wringing his long hair with great composure.

'I have mentioned this boatman repeatedly as an old man, and such he was to all appearance; his hair was grey, his face wrinkled, his back bent, and all his limbs and features had the appearance of those of a man of sixty, yet his real age was but twenty-seven years. He told me that he was the oldest boatman on the Rhone; that his younger brothers had been worn out before they were twenty-five years old.'

The French society at Lyons included many agreeable people; but Edgeworth singles out from among them, as his special friend, the Marquis de la Poype, who understood English, and was well acquainted with English literature. He pressed Edgeworth to pay him a visit at his Château in Dauphiny, and the latter adds: 'I promised to pass with him some of the Christmas holidays. An English gentleman went with me. We arrived in the evening at a very antique building, surrounded by a moat, and with gardens laid out in the style which was common in England in the beginning of the last century. These were enclosed by high walls, intersected by canals, and cut into parterres by sandy walks. We were ushered into a good drawing-room, the walls of which

were furnished with ancient tapestry. When dinner
was served, we crossed a large and lofty hall, that
was hung round with armour, and with the spoils of
the chase ; we passed into a moderate-sized eating-
room, in which there was no visible fireplace, but
which was sufficiently heated by invisible stoves.
The want of the cheerful light of a fire cast a gloom
over our repast, and the howling of the wind did not
contribute to lessen this dismal effect.   But the
dinner was good, and the wine, which was produced
from the vineyard close to the house, was excellent.
Madame de la Poype, and two or three of her friends,
who were on a visit at her house, conversed agreeably, and all feeling of winter and seclusion was
forgotten.

'At night, when I was shown into my chamber, the
footman asked if I chose to have my bed warmed.
I inquired whether it was well aired ; he assured me,
with a tone of integrity, that I had nothing to fear, for
"that it had not been slept in for half a year."   The
French are not afraid of damp beds, but they have a
great dread of catching some infectious disease from
sleeping in any bed in which a stranger may have
recently lain.

'My bedchamber at this château was hung with
tapestry, and as the footman assured me of the safety
of my bed, he drew aside a piece of the tapestry, which

discovered a small recess in the wall that held a *grabat*, in which my servant was invited to repose. My servant was an Englishman, whose indignation nothing but want of words to express it could have concealed ; he deplored my unhappy lot ; as for himself, he declared, with a look of horror, that nothing could induce him to go into such a pigeon-hole. I went to visit the accommodations of my companion, Mr. Rosenhagen. I found him in a spacious apartment hung all round with tapestry, so that there was no appearance of any windows. I was far from being indifferent to the comfort of a good dry bed ; but poor Mr. Rosenhagen, besides being delicate, was hypochondriac. With one of the most rueful countenances I ever beheld, he informed me that he must certainly *die* of cold. His teeth chattered whilst he pointed to the tapestry at one end of the room, which waved to and fro with the wind ; and, looking behind it, I found a large, stone casement window without a single pane of glass, or shutters of any kind. He determined not to take off his clothes ; but I, gaining courage from despair, undressed, went to bed, and never slept better in my life, or ever awakened in better health or spirits than at ten o'clock the next morning.

'After breakfast the Marquis took us to visit the Grotto de la Baume, which was at the distance of not

more than two leagues from his house. We were
most hospitably received at the house of an old
officer, who was *Seigneur* of the place. His hall was
more amply furnished with implements of the chase
and spoils of the field than any which I have ever
seen, or ever heard described. There were nets of
such dimensions, and of such strength, as were quite
new to me; bows, cross-bows, of prodigious power;
guns of a length and weight that could not be wielded
by the strength of modern arms; some with old
matchlocks, and with rests to be stuck into the
ground, and others with wheel-locks; besides modern
fire-arms of all descriptions; horns of deer, and tusks
of wild boars, were placed in compartments in such
numbers, that every part of the walls was covered
either with arms or trophies.

'The master of the mansion, in bulk, dress, and
general appearance, was suited to the style of life
which might be expected from what we had seen at
our entrance. He was above six feet high, strong,
and robust, though upwards of sixty years of age; he
wore a leather jerkin, and instead of having his hair
powdered, and tied in a long queue, according to the
fashion of the day, he wore his own short grey locks;
his address was plain, frank, and hearty, but by no
means coarse or vulgar. He was of an ancient family,
but of a moderate fortune.'   Here Edgeworth adds a

long description of the grotto and its stalactites. They returned to dine with the old officer at his castle.

'Our dinner was in its arrangement totally unlike anything I had seen in France, or anywhere else. It consisted of a monstrous, but excellent, wild boar ham ; this, and a large savoury pie of different sorts of game, were the principal dishes ; which, with some common vegetables, amply satisfied our hunger. The blunt hospitality of this rural baron was totally different from that which is to be met with in remote parts of the country of England. It was more the open-heartedness of a soldier than the roughness of a squire.'

During the winter of 1772 Edgeworth was busy making plans for flour-mills to be erected on a piece of land gained from the river. But his stay in Lyons was cut short as the news reached him in March 1773 that Mrs. Edgeworth, who had returned to England for her confinement, had died after giving birth to a daughter. He travelled home with his son through Burgundy and Paris, and on reaching England arranged to meet Mr. Day at Woodstock. His friend greeted him with the words, ' Have you heard anything of Honora Sneyd ? '

Mr. Edgeworth continues : ' I assured him that I had heard nothing but what he had told me when he was in France; that she had some disease in her eyes, and that it was feared she would lose her sight.' I added that I was resolved to offer her my hand, even if she had undergone such a dreadful privation.

'"My dear friend," said he, "while virtue and honour forbade you to think of her, I did everything in my power to separate you; but now that you are both at liberty, I have used the utmost expedition to reach you on your arrival in England, that I might be the first to tell you that Honora is in perfect health and beauty, improved in person and in mind; and, though surrounded by lovers, still her own mistress."

' At this moment I enjoyed the invaluable reward of my steady adherence to the resolution which I had formed on leaving England, never to keep up the slightest intercourse with her by letter, message, or inquiry. I enjoyed also the proof my friend gave me of his generous affection. Mr. Day had now come several hundred miles for the sole purpose of telling me of the fair prospects before me. . . .

' A new era in my life was now beginning. . . . I went directly to Lichfield, to Dr. Darwin's. The doctor was absent, but his sister, an elderly maiden lady, who then kept house for him, received me kindly.

'"You will excuse me," said the good lady, "for not making tea for you this evening, as I am engaged to the Miss Sneyds; but perhaps you will accompany me, as I am sure you will be welcome."

'It was summer—We found the drawing-room at Mr. Sneyd's filled by all my former acquaintances and friends, who had, without concert among themselves, assembled as if to witness the meeting of two persons, whose sentiments could scarcely be known even to the parties themselves.

'I have been told that the last person whom I addressed or saw, when I came into the room, was Honora Sneyd. This I do not remember; but I am perfectly sure that, when I did see her, she appeared to me most lovely, even more lovely than when we parted. What her sentiments might be it was impossible to divine.

'My addresses were, after some time, permitted and approved; and, with the consent of her father, Miss Honora Sneyd and I were married (1773), by special licence, in the ladies' choir, in the Cathedral at Lichfield. Immediately after the marriage ceremony we left Lichfield, and went to Ireland.'

Now followed what was perhaps the happiest period of Mr. Edgeworth's life, but it was uneventful. The young couple saw little society while living at Edgeworth Town; and after a three years' residence in Ireland, they visited England to rub off the rust of isolation in contact with their intellectual friends.

He says : 'We certainly found a considerable change for the better as to comfort, convenience, and conversation among our English acquaintance. So much so, that we were induced to remain in England. . . . My mind was kept up to the current of speculation and discovery in the world of science, and continual hints for reflection and invention were suggested to me. . . . My attention was about this period turned to clockwork, and I invented several pieces of mechanism for measuring time. These, with the assistance of a good workman, I executed successfully. I then (in 1776) finished a clock on a new construction. Its accuracy was tried at the Observatory at Oxford . . . and it is now (in 1809) going well at my house in Ireland.'

Edgeworth now enjoyed the pleasure of having an intelligent companion, and says : 'My wife had an eager desire for knowledge of all sorts, and, perhaps to please me, became an excellent theoretic mechanic. Mechanical amusements occupied my mornings, and I dedicated my evenings to the best books upon various subjects. I strenuously endeavoured to improve my own understanding, and to communicate whatever I knew to my wife. Indeed, while we read and conversed together during the long winter evenings, the clearness of her judgment assisted me in every pursuit of literature in which I was engaged ; as her understanding had arrived at maturity before she had acquired any strong prejudices on historical subjects, she derived uncommon advantage from books.

'We had frequent visitors from town ; and as our acquaintance were people of literature and science, conversation with them exercised and arranged her thoughts upon whatever subject they were employed. Nor did we neglect the education of our children : Honora had under her care, at this time, two children of her own, and three of mine by my former marriage.'

Edgeworth and his friend Mr. Day were both great admirers of Rousseau's *Émile* and of his scheme of bringing up children to be hardy, fearless, and independent. Edgeworth brought up his eldest boy after this fashion ; but though he succeeded in making him hardy, and training him in ' all the virtues of a child bred in the hut of a savage, and all the knowledge of *things* which could well be acquired at an early age by a boy bred in civilised society,' yet he adds : ' He was not disposed to *obey* ; his exertions generally arose from his own will; and, though he was what is commonly called good-tempered and good-natured, though he generally pleased by his looks, demeanour, and conversation, he had too little deference for others, and he showed an invincible dislike to control.'

In passing through Paris, Edgeworth and Mr. Day
went to see Rousseau, who took a good deal of notice
of Edgeworth's son; he judged him to be a boy of
abilities, and he thought from his answers that
'history can be advantageously learned by children,
if it be taught reasonably and not merely by rote.'
'But,' said Rousseau, 'I remark in your son a pro-
pensity to party prejudice, which will be a great
blemish in his character.'

'I asked how he could in so short a time form so
decided an opinion. He told me that, whenever my
son saw a handsome horse, or a handsome carriage
in the street, he always exclaimed, "That is an
English horse or an English carriage!" And that, even
down to a pair of shoe-buckles, everything that
appeared to be good of its kind was always pronounced by him to be English. "This sort of party
prejudice," said Rousseau, "if suffered to become a
ruling motive in his mind, will lead to a thousand
evils; for not only will his own country, his own
village or club, or even a knot of his private acquaintance, be the object of his exclusive admiration; but
he will be governed by his companions, whatever they
may be, and they will become the arbiters of his
destiny."'

It was while at Lyons that Edgeworth realised that
Rousseau's system of education was not altogether

satisfactory. He says: 'I had begun his education upon the mistaken principles of Rousseau; and I had pursued them with as much steadiness, and, so far as they could be advantageous, with as much success as I could desire. Whatever regarded the health, strength, and agility of my son had amply justified the system of my master; but I found myself entangled in difficulties with regard to my child's mind and temper. He was generous, brave, good-natured, and what is commonly called good-tempered; but he was scarcely to be controlled. It was difficult to urge him to anything that did not suit his fancy, and more difficult to restrain him from what he wished to follow. In short, he was self-willed, from a spirit of independence, which had been inculcated by his early education, and which he cherished the more from the inexperience of his own powers.

'I must here acknowledge, with deep regret, not only the error of a theory, which I had adopted at a very early age, when older and wiser persons than myself had been dazzled by the eloquence of Rousseau; but I must also reproach myself with not having, after my arrival in France, paid as much attention to my boy as I had done in England, or as much as was necessary to prevent the formation of those habits, which could never afterwards be eradicated.'

Edgeworth, finding that the tutor he had brought from England was not able to control his son, resolved to send young Richard to school at Lyons. The Jesuits had lately been dismissed, but the Pères de l'Oratoire had taken charge of their Seminary, and to them Edgeworth resolved to intrust his son, having been first assured by the Superior that he would not attempt to convert the boy, and would forbid the under-masters to do so. A certain Père Jerome, however, desired to make the boy a good Catholic ; and the Superior frankly told Edgeworth the circumstance, saying, ' One day he took your boy between his knees, and began from the beginning of things to teach him what he ought to believe. " My little man," said he, " did you ever hear of God ? "

' " Yes. '

' " You know that, before He made the world, His Spirit brooded over the vast deep, which was a great sea without shores, and *without bottom.* Then He made this world out of earth."

' " Where did He find the *earth* ? " asked the boy.

' " At the bottom of the sea," replied Father Jerome.

' " But," said the boy, " you told me just now that the sea had no bottom ! " '

The Superior of the Collége des Oratoires concluded, ' You may, sir, I think, be secure that your son, when capable of making such a reply, is in no great danger of becoming a Catholic from the lectures of such profound teachers as these.'

This son, having no turn for scholarship, ultimately went to sea, a life which his hardihood and fearlessness of danger peculiarly fitted him for. Some years afterwards he married an American lady and settled in South Carolina.

It was, perhaps, a failure in this first experiment in education which made Edgeworth devote so much care to the training of his younger children.

CHAPTER IV

AFTER six years of happiness Honora's health gave way, and consumption set in ; some months of anxious nursing followed before she died, to the great grief of her husband. She left several children, and her dying wish was that he should marry her sister Elizabeth.

Mr. Edgeworth was, at first, benumbed by grief, and unable to take an interest in his former pursuits ; but in the society of his wife's family he gradually recovered cheerfulness, and began to consider his wife's dying advice to marry her sister. He remarks : ' Nothing is more erroneous than the common belief, that a man who has lived in the greatest happiness with one wife will be the most averse to take another. On the contrary, the loss of happiness, which he feels when he loses her, necessarily urges him to endeavour to be again placed in a situation which has constituted his former felicity.

' I felt that Honora had judged wisely, and from a thorough knowledge of my character, when she had advised me to marry again.'

After these observations it is not surprising to hear
that Edgeworth became engaged to Elizabeth Sneyd
in the autumn of 1780. They were staying for the
marriage at Brereton Hall in Cheshire, and their
banns were published in the parish church; but on
the very morning appointed for the marriage, the
clergyman received a letter which roused so many
scruples in his mind as to make Edgeworth think it
cruel to press him to perform the ceremony. The
Rector of St. Andrew's, Holborn, was less scrupulous,
and they were married there on Christmas Day 1780.

The following summer Mr. and Mrs. Edgeworth
rented Davenport Hall in Cheshire, where they lived
a quiet retired life, spending a good deal of their time
with their friends Sir Charles and Lady Holte at
Brereton. Edgeworth amused himself by making a
clock for the steeple at Brereton, and a chronometer
of a singular construction, which, he says, ' I intended
to present to the King . . . to add to His Majesty's
collection of uncommon clocks and watches which I
had seen at St. James's.'

The autobiography from which I have been quoting
was begun by Edgeworth when he was about sixty-
three, and it breaks off abruptly at the date of 1781.
The illness which interrupted his task did not, however,
prove fatal, for he lived nearly ten years afterwards.

His daughter Maria takes up the narrative, and in

her introduction she says, 'In continuing these *Memoirs*, I shall endeavour to follow the example that my father has set me of simplicity and of truth.'

The following memorandum was found in Edgeworth's handwriting : 'In the year 1782 I returned to Ireland, with a firm determination to dedicate the remainder of my life to the improvement of my estate, and to the education of my children ; and farther, with the sincere hope of contributing to the amelioration of the inhabitants of the country from which I drew my subsistence.'

When in the spring of 1768 Edgeworth visited Ireland with his friend Mr. Day, the latter was surprised and disgusted by the state of Dublin and of the country in general.   He found 'the streets of Dublin were wretchedly paved, and more dirty than can be easily imagined.' Edgeworth adds : 'As we passed through the country, the hovels in which the poor were lodged, which were then far more wretched than they are at present, or than they have been for the last twenty years, the black tracts of bog, and the unusual smell of the turf fuel, were to him never-ceasing topics of reproach and lamentation. Mr. Day's deep-seated prejudice in favour of savage life was somewhat shaken by this view of want and misery, which philosophers of a certain class in London and Paris chose at that time to dignify by the name of simplicity. The modes of living in the houses of the gentry were much the same in Ireland as in England. This surprised my friend. He observed, that if there was any difference, it was that people of similar fortune did not restrain themselves equally in both countries to the same prudent economy; but that every gentleman in Ireland, of two or three thousand pounds a year, lived in a certain degree of luxury and show that would be thought presumptuous in persons of the same fortune in England.

'On our journey to my father's house, I had occasion to vote at a contested election in one of the counties through which we passed. Here a scene of noise, riot, confusion, and drunkenness was exhibited, not superior indeed in depravity and folly, but of a character or manner so different from what my friend had even seen in his own country, that he fell into a profound melancholy.'

It was to remedy this wretched state of things in Ireland that Edgeworth resolved in 1782 to devote his energies.

It is curious to read his account of the relations between landlord and tenant in Ireland at this date. He soon learned that firmness was required in his dealings with his tenants as well as kindness. 'He omitted a variety of old feudal remains of fines and penalties; but there was one clause, which he continued

in every lease with a penalty attached to it, called *an
alienation fine*—a fine of so much an acre upon the
tenant's reletting any part of the devised land.'

He wisely resolved to receive his rents himself, and
to avoid the intervention of any agent or *driver* ('a
person who drives and impounds cattle for rent or
arrears'). 'In every case where the tenant had
improved the land, or even where he had been
industrious, though unsuccessful, his claim to preference over every new proposer, his *tenant's right*, as it
is called, was admitted. But the mere plea of "*I
have lived under your Honour, or your Honour's father
or grandfather,*" or "*I have been on your Honour's estate
so many years,*" he disregarded. Farms, originally
sufficient for the comfortable maintenance of a man,
his wife, and family, had in many cases, been sub-
divided from generation to generation, the father
giving a bit of the land to each son to settle him. It
was an absolute impossibility that the land should
ever be improved if let in these miserable *lots*. Nor
was it necessary that each son should hold land, or
advantageous that each should live on *his* "*little potato
garden,*" without further exertion of mind or body.

'There was a continual struggle between landlord
and tenant upon the question of long and short
leases. . . . The offer of immediate high rent, or of
fines to be paid down directly, tempted the landlord's

extravagance, or supplied his present necessities, at
the expense of his future interests. . . . Many have
let for ninety-nine years; and others, according to a
form common in Ireland, for three lives, renewable
for ever, paying a small fine on the insertion of a new
life at the failure of each. These leases, in course of
years, have been found extremely disadvantageous to
the landlord, the property having risen so much in value
that the original rent was absurdly disproportioned.

'The longest term my father ever gave,' says his
daughter Maria, 'was thirty-one years, with one or
sometimes two lives. He usually gave one life, re-
serving to himself the option of adding another—the
son, perhaps, of the tenant—if he saw that the tenant
deserved it by his conduct. This sort of power to
encourage and reward in the hands of a landlord is
advantageous in Ireland. It acts as a motive for
exertion; it keeps up the connection and dependence
which there ought to be between the different ranks,
without creating any servile habits, or leaving the
improving tenant insecure as to the fair reward of his
industry.

'Edgeworth's plan was to take not that which,
abstractedly viewed, is the best possible course, but
that which is the best the circumstances will altogether allow.

'When the oppressive duty-work in Ireland was no

longer claimed, and no longer inserted in Irish
leases, there arose a difficulty to gentlemen in getting
labourers at certain times of the year, when all are
anxious to work for themselves; for instance, at the
seasons for cutting turf, setting potatoes, and getting
home the harvest.

'To provide against this difficulty, landlords adopted
a system of taking duty-work, in fact, in a new form.
They had *cottiers* (cottagers), day-labourers established in cottages, on their estate, usually near their
own residence. Many of these cabins were the poorest
habitations that can be imagined; and these were
given *rent free*, that is, the rent was to be *worked* out
on whatever days, or on whatever occasions, it was
called for. The grazing for *the* cow, the patch of land
for flax, and the ridge or ridges of potato land were
also to be paid for in days' labour in the same
manner. The uncertainty of this tenure *at will*, that
is, at the pleasure of the landlord, with the rent in
labour and time, variable also at his pleasure or convenience, became rather more injurious to the tenant
than the former fixed mode of sacrificing so many
days' duty-work, even at the most hazardous seasons
of the year.

' My father wished to have entirely avoided this
cottager system; but he was obliged to adopt a
middle course. To his labourers he gave comfortable

cottages at a low rent, to be held at will from year to year; but he paid them wages exactly the same as what they could obtain elsewhere. Thus they were partly free and partly bound. They worked as free labourers; but they were obliged to work, that they might pay their rent. And their houses being better, and other advantages greater, than they could obtain elsewhere, they had a motive for industry and punctuality; thus their services and their attachment were properly secured. . . . My father's indulgence as to the time he allowed his tenantry for the payment of their rent was unusually great. He left always a year's rent in their hands: this was half a year more time than almost any other gentleman in our part of the country allowed. . . . He was always very exact in requiring that the rents should not, in their payments, pass beyond the half-yearly days—the 25th of March and 29th of September. In this point they knew his strictness so well that they seldom ventured to go into arrear, and never did so with impunity. . . . They would have cheated, loved, and despised a more easy landlord, and his property would have gone to ruin, without either permanently bettering their interests or their morals. He, therefore, took especial care that they should be convinced of his strictness in punishing as well as of his desire to reward.

D

'Where the offender was tenant, and the punisher
landlord, it rarely happened, even if the law reached
the delinquent, that public opinion sided with public
justice.   In Ireland it has been, time immemorial,
common with tenants, who have had advantageous
bargains, and who have no hopes of getting their
leases renewed, to waste the ground as much as
possible ; to *break it up* towards the end of the term ;
or to *overhold*, that is, to keep possession of the
land, refusing to deliver it up.

'A tenant, who held a farm of considerable value,
when his lease was out, besought my father to permit him to remain on the farm for another year,
pleading that he had no other place to which he
could, at that season, it being winter, remove his large
family.   The permission was granted ; but at the end
of the year, taking advantage of this favour, he refused to give up the land.   Proceedings at law were
immediately commenced against him ; and it was in
this case that the first trial in Ireland was brought,
on an act for recovering double rent from a tenant
for holding forcible possession after notice to quit.

'This vexatious and unjust practice of tenants
against landlords had been too common, and had too
long been favoured by the party spirit of juries ; who,
being chiefly composed of tenants, had made it a
common cause, and a principle, if it could in any way

be avoided, never to give a verdict, as they said, against themselves. But in this case the indulgent character of the landlord, combined with the ability and eloquence of his advocate, succeeded in moving the jury—a verdict was obtained for the landlord. The double rent was paid ; and the fraudulent tenant was obliged to quit the country *unpitied*. Real good was done by this example.'

Edgeworth objected strongly to a practice common among the gentry, ' *to protect* their tenants when they got into any difficulties by disobeying the laws. Smuggling and illicit distilling seemed to be privileged cases, where, the justice and expediency of the spirit of the law being doubtful, escaping from the letter of it appeared but a trial of ingenuity or *luck*. In cases that admitted of less doubt, in the frequent breach of the peace from quarrels at fairs, rescuing of cattle drivers for rent, or in other more serious outrages, tenants still looked to their landlord for protection ; and hoped, even to the last, that his Honour's or his Lordship's interest would get the fine taken off, the term of imprisonment shortened, or the condemned criminal snatched from execution. He [Edgeworth] never would, on any occasion, or for the persons he was known to like best, interfere to *protect*, as it is called, that is, to screen, or to obtain pardon for any one of his tenants or dependants, if they had really infringed the laws, or had deserved punishment. . . . He set an example of being scrupulous to the most exact degree as a grand juror, both as to the money required for roads or for any public works, and as to the manner in which it was laid out.

'To his character as a good landlord was soon added that he was a *real gentleman*. This phrase, pronounced with well-known emphasis, comprises a great deal in the opinion of the lower Irish. They seem to have an instinct for the *real gentleman*, whom they distinguish, if not at first sight, infallibly at first hearing, from every pretender to the character. They observe that the real gentleman bears himself most kindly, is always the most civil in speech, and ever seems the most *tender of the poor*. . . .

'They soon began to rely upon his justice as a magistrate. This is a point where, their interest being nearly concerned, they are wonderfully quick and clearsighted ; they soon discovered that Mr. Edgeworth leaned neither to Protestant nor Catholic, to Presbyterian nor Methodist ; that he was not the *favourer* nor partial protector of his own or any other man's followers. They found that the law of the land was not in his hands an instrument of oppression, or pretence for partiality. They discerned that he did even justice ; neither inclining to the people, for the sake of popularity ; nor to the aristocracy, for the sake of power. This was a thing so unusual, that they could at first hardly believe that it was really what they saw.

'Soon after his return to Ireland he set about improving a considerable tract of land, reletting it at an advanced rent, which gave the actual monied measure of his skill and success.' He also wrote a paper on the draining and planting of bogs, in which he gives minute directions for carrying out the work, for he was no mere theorist, but experimented on his own property; and he was not ashamed to own when he had made a mistake, but was constantly learning from experience.

He had for a while to turn from peaceful occupations and take his share in patriotic efforts for parliamentary reform; this reform was pressed on the parliament sitting in Dublin by a delegation from a convention of the Irish volunteers. They were raised in 1778 during the American War, when England had not enough troops for the defence of Ireland. The principal Irish nobility and gentry enrolled themselves, and the force at length increased, till it numbered 50,000 men, under the command of officers of their own choosing. The Irish patriots now felt their power, and used it with prudence and energy. They obtained the repeal of many noxious laws—one in particular was a penal statute passed in the reign of William III. against the Catholics ordaining forfeiture of inheritance against those Catholics who had been educated abroad. 'At the pleasure of any informer, it confiscated their estates to the next Protestant heir ; that statute further deprived Papists of the power of obtaining any legal property by purchase ; and, simply for officiating in the service of his religion, any Catholic priest was liable to be imprisoned for life. Some of these penalties had fallen into disuse ; but, as Mr. Dunning stated to the English House of Commons, "many respectable Catholics still lived in fear of them, and some actually paid contributions to persons who, on the strength of this act, threatened them with prosecutions." Lord Shelburne stated in the House of Lords "that even the most odious part of this statute had been recently acted upon in the case of one Moloury, an Irish priest, who had been informed against, apprehended, convicted, and committed to prison, by means of the lowest and most despicable of mankind, a common informing constable. The Privy Council used efforts in behalf of the prisoner ; but, in consequence of the written law, the King himself could not give a pardon, and the prisoner must have died in jail if Lord Shelburne and his colleagues had not released him at their own risk."'

This law was repealed by the English House of

Commons without a negative, and only one Bishop opposed its repeal in the House of Lords.

Having won this victory, the Irish patriots continued their campaign, and now sought to win general emancipation from the legislative and commercial restrictions of England. It was in 1781 that the first convention of volunteer delegates met, and some months after Mr. Grattan moved an address to the throne asserting the legislative independence of Ireland. 'The address passed ; the repeal of a certain act, empowering England to legislate for Ireland, followed; and the legislative independence of this country was acknowledged.'

Edgeworth sympathised with the enthusiasm which prevailed throughout Ireland at this time; but he was shrewd enough to see that what was further required for the real benefit of the country was 'an effectual reformation of the Irish House of Commons.'

The counties were insufficiently represented, and the boroughs were venal. The Irish parliament was, in fact, an Oligarchy, and Edgeworth realised this danger. He, however, wished the reform to be carried on 'through the intervention of parliament,' while the more extreme party insisted on sending delegates from the volunteers to a convention in Dublin. This military convention 'met at the Royal Exchange in Dublin, November the 9th, 1783.

—Parliament was then sitting. An armed convention assembled in the capital, and sitting at the same time with the Houses of Lords and Commons, deliberating on a legislative question, was a new and unprecedented spectacle.

'In this convention, as in all public assemblies, there was a violent and a moderate party. Lord Charlemont, the president of the assembly, was at the head of the moderate men. Though not convinced of the strict legality of the meeting, he thought a reform in parliament so important and desirable an object, that to the probability or chance of obtaining this great advantage it was the wisdom of a true patriot to sacrifice punctilio, and to hazard all, but, what he was too wise and good to endanger, the peace of the country. Lord Charlemont accepted the office of president, specially with the hope that he and his friends might be able to influence the convention in favour of proceedings at once temperate and firm. The very sincerity of his desire to attain a reform rendered him clear-sighted as to the means to be pursued; and while he wished that the people should be allowed every degree of liberty consistent with safety, no man was less inclined to democracy, or could feel more horror at the idea of involving his country in a state of civil anarchy.

'The Bishop of Derry (Lord Bristol), wishing well

to Ireland, but of a far less judicious character than
Lord Charlemont, was at the head of the opposite
party. . . . Lord Charlemont, foreseeing the danger
of disagreement between the parliament and convention, if at this time any communication were opened
between them, earnestly deprecated the attempts. It
was his desire that the convention, after declaring
their opinion in favour of a parliamentary reform,
should adjourn without adopting a specific plan;
and that they should refer it to future meetings of
each county, to send to parliament, in the regular
constitutional manner, their petitions and addresses.
Mr. Flood, however, whose abilities and eloquence
had predominant influence over the convention, and
who wished to distinguish himself in parliament as
the proposer of reform, prevailed upon the convention,
on one of the last nights of their meeting, to send
him, accompanied by other members of parliament
from among the volunteer delegates, directly to the
House of Commons then sitting. There he was to
make a motion on the question of parliamentary
reform, introducing to the House his specific plan
from the convention. The appearance of Mr. Flood,
and of the delegates by whom he was accompanied,
in their volunteer uniforms, in the Irish House of
Commons, excited an extraordinary sensation. Those
who were present, and who have given an account of

the scene that ensued, describe it as violent and tumultuous in the extreme. On both sides the passions were worked up to a dangerous height. The debate lasted all night. " The *tempest*, for, towards morning, *debate* there was none, at last ceased." The question was put, and Mr. Flood's motion for reform in parliament was negatived by a very large majority. The House of Commons then entered into resolutions declaratory of their fixed determination to maintain their just rights and privileges against any encroachments whatever, adding *that it was at that time indispensably necessary to make such a declaration.* Further, an address was moved, intended to be made the joint address of Lords and Commons to the throne, expressing their satisfaction with His Majesty's Government, and their resolution to support that government, and the constitution, *with their lives and fortunes.* The address was carried up to the Lords, and immediately agreed to. This was done with the celerity of passion on all sides.

' Meantime an armed convention continued sitting the whole night, waiting for the return of their delegates from the House of Commons, and impatient to learn the fate of Mr. Flood's motion. One step more, and irreparable, fatal imprudence might have been committed. Lord Charlemont, the president of the convention, felt the danger; and it required all the

influence of his character, all the assistance of the
friends of moderation, to prevail upon the assembly
to dissolve, without waiting longer to hear the report
from their delegates in the House of Commons. The
convention had, in fact, nothing more to do, or
nothing that they could attempt without peril ; but
it was difficult to persuade the assembly to dissolve
the meeting, and to return quietly to their respective
counties and homes. This point, however, was fortunately accomplished, and early in the morning the
meeting terminated.'

Miss Edgeworth adds : 'I have heard my father
say that he ever afterwards rejoiced in the share
he had in preserving one of the chiefs of this
volunteer convention from a desperate resolution,
and in determining the assembly to a temperate
termination.'

Writing of this convention many years afterwards,
Edgeworth says : 'There never was any assembly in
the British empire more in earnest in the business
on which they were convened, or less influenced by
courtly interference or cabal. But the object was in
itself unattainable.

'The idea of admitting Roman Catholics to the
right of voting for representatives was not urged
even by the most liberal and most enlightened
members of the convention ; and the number,

and wealth, and knowledge of Protestant voters in Ireland could not decently be considered as sufficient to elect an adequate and fair representation of the people.'

The reforms were never carried, though fresh efforts, equally unsuccessful, were made when Pitt became minister.

CHAPTER V

IT was in 1786 that Edgeworth had a severe fall from a scaffolding, the result of which was, as his friend Dr. Darwin prophesied, an attack of jaundice. When the workmen brought him home, he tried to reassure his family by telling them the story of a French *Marquis*, 'who fell from a balcony at Versailles, and who, as it was court politeness that nothing unfortunate should ever be mentioned in the King's presence, replied to His Majesty's inquiry if he wasn't hurt by his fall, " *Tout au contraire, Sire.*"' To all our inquiries whether he was hurt, my father replied, ' *Tout au contraire, mes amies.*'

His friendship for Mr. Day, which had existed for many years, was now interrupted by Mr. Day's sudden death from a fall from his horse in 1789. Edgeworth thought of writing his life, as he considered him to have been a man of such original an and noble character as to deserve a public eulogium. He goes on to say: 'To preserve a portrait to posterity, it must either be the likeness of some celebrated individual,

or it must represent a face which, independently of
peculiar associations, corresponds with the universal
ideas of beauty. So the pen of the biographer should
portray only those who by their public have interested
us in their private characters; or who, in a superior
degree, have possessed the virtues and mental endow-
ments which claim the general love and admiration
of mankind.' This biography, however, was never
finished, as Edgeworth found another friend, Mr. Keir,
had undertaken it; he therefore sent the materials to
him, but some of them are incorporated in the *Memoirs*.
Sabrina, whom Mr. Day had educated, and intended
to marry (though he gave up the idea when he doubted
her docility and power of adaptiveness to his strange
theories of life), ultimately married his friend, Mr.
Bicknel, while Mr. Day married Miss Milne, a clever
and accomplished lady, who had sufficient tact to fall
in with his wishes, and a wifely devotion which made
up to her for their seclusion from general society. In
her widowhood she found Mr. Edgeworth a most
faithful and helpful friend; he offered to come over
and aid in the search which was made at Mr. Day's
death for a large sum of money which was not forth-
coming, and which it was thought he might, after his
eccentric fashion, have concealed; as he took this
measure when, 'at the time of the American War,
he had apprehended that there would have been a

national bankruptcy, and under this dread he had sold out of the Stocks. . . . A very considerable sum had been buried under the floor of the study in his mother's house. This he afterwards took up, and placed again in the public funds at the return of peace.'

Mr. Day had, before his marriage, promised to leave his library to his friend Edgeworth, but no mention was made of this in the will; he left almost everything to Mrs. Day. She, however, hearing of Mr. Day's promise, offered his library to his friend; but Edgeworth, in the same generous spirit, refused it, and Mrs. Day then wrote to him as follows:—

'MY DEAR MR. EDGEWORTH,—I will ingenuously own, that of all the bequests Mr. Day could have made, the leaving his whole library from me would have mortified me the most—indeed, more than if he had disposed of all his other property, and left me only that. My ideas of him are so much associated with his books, that to part with them would be, as it were, breaking some of the last ties which still connect me with so beloved an object. The being in the midst of books he has been accustomed to read, and which contain his marks and notes, will still give him a sort of *existence* with *me*. Unintelligible as such fond chimeras may appear to many people, I am persuaded they are not so to you.'

Maria Edgeworth adds : ' Generous people understand each other. Mrs Day, of a noble disposition
herself, always distinguished in my father the same
generosity of disposition. She had, she said, ever
considered him as "the most purely disinterested and
proudly independent of Mr. Day's friends."'

Edgeworth was a devoted father ; and the loss of
his daughter Honora, a gifted girl of fifteen, was a great
blow to him. She was the child of his beloved wife
Honora, and he had taken great pleasure in guiding
her studies and watching the development of her
character. Ever since he had settled in his Irish
home one of Edgeworth's chief interests had been
the education of his large family ; Maria records with
pride that at the age of seven Honora was able to
answer the following questions :—

' If a line move its own length through the air so
as to produce a surface, what figure will it describe?'

She answered, ' A *square.*'

She was then asked—

' If that square be moved downwards or upwards
in the air the space of the length of one of its own
sides, what figure will it, at the end of its motion,
have described in the air?'

After a few minutes' silence she answered, ' A *cube.*'

Edgeworth was careful to train not only the
reasoning powers, but also the imaginative faculty of

his children; he delighted in good poetry and fiction, and read aloud well, and his daughter writes : ' From the Arabian Tales to Shakespeare, Milton, Homer, and the Greek tragedians, all were associated in the minds of his children with the delight of hearing passages from them first read by their father.'

He was an enthusiastic admirer of the ancient classics—Homer and the Greek tragedians in particular. From the best translations of the ancient tragedies he selected for reading aloud the most striking passages, and Pope's 'Iliad' and 'Odyssey' he read several times to his family, in certain portions every day.

In his grief for his child, Edgeworth turned to his earliest friend, his sister, the favourite companion of his childhood, and from her he received all the consolation that affectionate sympathy could give; but, as he said, 'for real grief there is no sudden cure ; all *human* resource is in time and occupation.'

It was about this time that Darwin published the now forgotten poem, 'The Botanic Garden,' and Edgeworth wrote to his friend expressing his admiration for it ; but Maria adds : ' With as much sincerity as he gave praise, my father blamed and opposed whatever he thought was faulty in his friend's poem. Dr. Darwin had formed a false theory, that *poetry is painting to the eye*; this led him to confine his atten-

E

tion to the language of description, or to the representation of that which would produce good effect in picture. To this one mistaken opinion he sacrificed the more lasting and more extensive fame, which he might have ensured by exercising the powers he possessed of rousing the passions and pleasing the imagination.

'When my father found that it was in vain to combat a favourite false principle, he endeavoured to find a subject which should at once suit his friend's theory and his genius. He urged him to write a "Cabinet of Gems." The ancient gems would have afforded a subject eminently suited to his descriptive powers. . . . The description of Medea, and of some of the labours of Hercules, etc., which he has introduced into his "Botanic Garden," show how admirably he would have succeeded had he pursued this plan ; and I cannot help regretting that the suggestions of his friend could not prevail upon him to quit for nobler objects his vegetable loves.'

Edgeworth's prediction has not yet come true, nor does it seem likely that it ever will, 'that in future times some critic will arise, who shall re-discover the "Botanic Garden,"' and build his fame upon this discovery.

Dr. Darwin did not follow his friend's advice, to choose a better subject for his next poem ; nor did

Edgeworth do what his friend wished, which was to publish a decade of inventions with neat maps.

In the education of his children, he had already learned the value of the observation of children's ways and mental states. Having found that Rousseau's system was imperfect, he was groping after some better method. His daughter writes: ' Long before he ever thought of writing or publishing, he had kept a register of observations and facts relative to his children. This he began in the year 1798. He and Mrs. Honora Edgeworth kept notes of every circumstance which occurred worth recording. Afterwards Mrs. Elizabeth Edgeworth and he continued the same practice ; and in consequence of his earnest exhortations, I began in 1791 or 1792 to note down anecdotes of the children whom he was then educating. Besides these, I often wrote for my own amusement and instruction some of his conversation-lessons, as we may call them, with his questions and explanations, and the answers of the children. . . . To all who ever reflected upon education it must have occurred that facts and experiments were wanting in this department of knowledge, while assertions and theories abounded. I claim for my father the merit of having been the first to recommend, both by example and precept, what Bacon would call the experimental method in education. If I were obliged to rest on any single point my father's credit as a lover of truth, and his utility as a philanthropist and as a philosophical writer, it should be on his having made this first record of experiments in education. . . . In noting anecdotes of children, the greatest care must be taken that the pupils should not know that any such register is kept. Want of care in this particular would totally defeat the object in view, and would lead to many and irremediable bad consequences, and would make the children affected and false, or would create a degree of embarrassment and constraint which must prevent the natural action of the understanding or the feelings. . . . In the registry of such observations, considered as contributing to a history of the human mind, nothing should be neglected as trivial. The circumstances which may seem most trifling to vulgar observers may be most valuable to the philosopher ; they may throw light, for example, on the manner in which ideas and language are formed and generalised.'

Edgeworth and his daughter Maria brought out their joint work, *Practical Education*, in 1798. Maria adds : ' So commenced that literary partnership, which for so many years was the pride and joy of my life.' We who were born in the first half of the nineteenth century can remember the delight of reading about Frank and Rosamund, and Harry and Lucy, and feel a debt of gratitude to the writers who gave us so many pleasant hours.

Edgeworth's patience in teaching was surprising, as Maria remarks, in a man of his vivacity. ' He would sit quietly while a child was thinking of the answer to a question without interrupting, or suffering it to be interrupted, and would let the pupil touch and quit the point repeatedly ; and without a leading observation or exclamation, he would wait till the steps of reasoning and invention were gone through, and were converted into certainties. . . . The tranquillising effect of this patience was of great advantage. The pupil's mind became secure, not only of the point in question, but steady in the confidence of its future powers. It was his principle to excite the attention fully and strongly for a short time, and *never to go to the point of fatigue.* . . . In the education of the heart, his warmth of approbation and strength of indignation had powerful and salutary influence in touching and developing the affections. The scorn in his countenance when he heard of any base conduct ; the pleasure that lighted up his eyes when he heard of any generous action ; the eloquence of his language, and vehemence of his emphasis, commanded the sympathy of all who could see, hear, feel, or understand. Added to the power of every moral or religious motive, sympathy with the virtuous enthusiasm of those we love and reverence produces a great and salutary effect.

'It often happens that a preceptor appears to have a great influence for a time, and that this power suddenly dissolves. This is, and must be the case, wherever any sort of deception has been used. My father never used any artifice of this kind, and consequently he always possessed that confidence, which is the reward of plain dealing—a confidence which increases in the pupil's mind with age, knowledge, and experience.'

The readers of the second part of 'Harry and Lucy' will remember the driving tour through England, which they took with their parents, who were careful to point out to them all that was of interest, and to rouse their powers of observation. And in the same manner Edgeworth, 'at the time when he was building or carrying on experiments, or work of any sort, constantly explained to his children whatever was done, and by his questions, adapted to their several ages and capacities, exercised their powers of observation, reasoning, and invention.

'It often happened that trivial circumstances, by which the curiosity of the children had been excited, or experiments obvious to the senses, by which they had been interested, led afterwards to deeper reflection or to philosophical inquiries, suited to others in the family of more advanced age and knowledge. The animation spread through the house by connecting children with all that is going on, and allowing them to join in thought or conversation with the grown-up people of the family, was highly useful, and thus both sympathy and emulation excited mental exertion in the most agreeable manner.'

In 1794 he wrote of his son Lovell : ' He has been employed in building and other active pursuits, which seldom fall to the share of young men, but which seem as agreeable to him as the occupations of a mail-coachman, a groom, or a stable-boy are to some youths. I am every day more convinced of the advantages of good education.' He adds : ' One of my younger boys is what is called a genius —that is to say, he has vivacity, attention, and good organs. I do not think one tear per month is shed in the house, nor the voice of reproof heard, nor the hand of restraint felt. To educate a second race costs no trouble. *Ce n'est que le premier pas qui coute.*'

The result of this watchful and tender interest in his children's education may be judged by a passage in the later part of the *Memoirs*, where his daughter says : ' When I was writing this page (July 1818), this brother was with me; and when I stopped to make some inquiry from him as to his recollection of that period of his life, he reminded me of many circumstances of my father's kindness to him, and brought to me letters written on his first entrance into the world, highly characteristic of the warmth of my father's affections, and of the strength of his mind. . . . The conviction is full and strong on my own mind, that a father's confiding kindness, and plain sincerity to a young man, when he first sets out in the world, make an impression the most salutary and indelible. When his sons first quitted the paternal roof, they were all completely at liberty ; he never took any indirect means to watch over or to influence them ; he treated them on all occasions with entire openness and confidence. In their tastes and pursuits, joys and sorrows, they were sure of their father's sympathy ; in all difficulties or disappointments, they applied to him, as their best friend, for counsel, consolation, or support ; and the delight that he took in any exertion of their talents, or in any instance of their honourable conduct, they felt as a constant generous excitement.'

Edgeworth had no ambition on his own account to be an author ; but his wish to supply wholesome literature for the young led him into writing, conjointly with his daughter, several books. Besides these was one which had a different object ; in the *Essay on Irish Bulls* he ' wished ' (his daughter writes) 'to show the English public the eloquence, wit, and talents of the lower classes of people in Ireland. . . . He excelled in imitating the Irish, because he never overstepped the modesty or the *assurance* of nature. He marked exquisitely the happy confidence, the shrewd wit of the people, without condescending to produce effect by caricature. He knew not only their comic talents, but their powers of pathos ; and often when he had just heard from them some pathetic complaint, he has repeated it to me while the impression was fresh. In the chapter on Wit and Eloquence in *Irish Bulls*, there is a speech of a poor freeholder to a candidate, who asked for his vote ; this speech was made to my father when he was canvassing the county of Longford. It was repeated to me a few hours afterwards, and I wrote it down instantly without, I believe, the variation of a word.

'In the same chapter there is the complaint of a poor widow against her landlord, and the landlord's reply in his own defence. This passage was quoted, I am told, by Campbell in one of his celebrated lectures on Eloquence. It was supposed by him to have been a quotation from a fictitious narrative, but, on the contrary, it is an unembellished fact. My father was the magistrate before whom the widow and her landlord appeared, and made that complaint and defence, which he repeated, and I may say acted,

for me. The speeches I instantly wrote word for
word, and the whole was described exactly from the
life of his representation.'

Edgeworth was anxious that his children should
have no unpleasant associations with their first steps
in reading; he therefore took great pains to find
out the easiest way of teaching them to read, and
wrote for this purpose *A Rational Primer*. Maria
adds : 'Nothing but the true desire to be useful could
have induced any man of talents to choose such in-
glorious labours; but he thought no labour, however
humble, beneath him, if it promised improvement
in education. . . . His principle of always giving
distinct marks for each different sound of the vowels
has been since brought into more general use. It
forms the foundation of Pestalozzi's plan of teaching
to read. But one of the most useful of the marks
in the *Rational Primer*, the mark of obliteration,
designed to show what letters are to be omitted in
pronouncing words, has not, I believe, been adopted
by any public instructor.'

Among the calls on Edgeworth's time about 1790
was the management of the embarrassed affairs of a
relation; he had some difficulties with the creditors,
but in trying to collect arrears of rent he found himself not only in difficulty, but in actual peril.

There existed in Ireland at this time a class of

persons calling themselves *gentlemen tenants*—the worst tenants in the world—*middlemen*, who relet the lands, and live upon the produce, not only in idleness, but in insolent idleness.

This kind of half gentry, or mock gentry, seemed to consider it as the most indisputable privilege of a gentleman not to pay his debts. They were ever ready to meet civil law with military brag of war. Whenever a swaggering debtor of this species was pressed for payment, he began by protesting or *confessing* that 'he considered himself used in an ungentlemanlike manner;' and ended by offering to give, instead of the value of his bond or promise, 'the *satisfaction* of a gentleman, at any hour or place. . . . My father,' says Maria, 'has often since rejoiced in the recollection of his steadiness at this period of his life. As far as the example of an individual could go, it was of service in his neighbourhood. It showed that such lawless proceedings as he had opposed *could* be effectually resisted ; and it discountenanced that braggadocio style of doing business which was once in Ireland too much in fashion.'

IT was in 1792 that Edgeworth left Ireland, and he and his family spent nearly two years at Clifton for the health of one of his sons. Maria writes: ' This was the first time I had ever been with him in what is called *the world* ; where he was not only a useful, but a most entertaining guide and companion. His observations upon characters, as they revealed themselves by slight circumstances, were amusing and just. He was a good judge of manners, and of all that related to appearance, both in men and women. Believing, as he did, that young people, from sympathy, imitate or catch involuntarily the habits and tone of the company they keep, he thought it of essential consequence that on their entrance into the world they should see the best models. " No company or good company," was his maxim. By *good* he did not mean *fine*. Airs and conceit he despised, as much as he disliked vulgarity. Affectation was under awe before him from an instinctive perception of his powers of ridicule. He could not endure, in favour of any pretensions of birth, fortune, or fashion, the stupidity of a formal circle, or the inanity of commonplace conversation. . . . Sometimes, perhaps, he went too far, and at this period of his life was too fastidious in his choice of society; or when he did go into mixed company, if he happened to be suddenly struck with any extravagance or meanness of fashion, he would inveigh against these with such vehemence as gave a false idea of his disposition. His auditors . . . were provoked to find that one, who could please in any company, should disdain theirs; and that he, who seemed made for society, should prefer living shut up with his own friends and family. An inconvenience arose from this, which is of more consequence than the mere loss of popularity, that he was not always known or understood by those who were really worthy of his acquaintance and regard.' His daughter says later: 'The whole style and tone of society (in Ireland) are altered.—The fashion has passed away of those desperately long, formal dinners, which were given two or three times a year by each family in the country to their neigh- bours, where the company had more than they could eat, and twenty times more than they should drink; where the gentlemen could talk only of claret, horses, or dogs; and the ladies, only of dress or scandal;

so that in the long hours, when they were left to their own discretion, after having examined and appraised each other's finery, many an absent neighbour's character was torn to pieces, merely for want of something to say or to do in the stupid circle. But now the dreadful circle is no more ; the chairs, which formerly could only take that form, at which the firmest nerves must ever tremble, are allowed to stand, or turn in any way which may suit the convenience and pleasure of conversation. The gentlemen and ladies are not separated from the time dinner ends till the midnight hour, when the carriages come to the door to carry off the bodies of the dead (drunk).

'A taste for reading and literary conversation has been universally acquired and diffused. Literature has become, as my father long ago prophesied that it would become, fashionable ; so that it is really necessary to all, who would appear to advantage, even in the society of their country neighbours.'

Referring to her father's conversational powers, Maria adds : 'His style in speaking and writing were as different as it is possible to conceive. In writing, cool and careful, as if on his guard against his natural liveliness of imagination ; he was so cautious to avoid exaggeration, that he sometimes repressed enthusiasm. The character of his writings, if I mistake not, is good sense ; the characteristic of his conversation was genius and vivacity—one moment playing on the surface, the next diving to the bottom of the subject. When anything touched his feelings, exciting either admiration or indignation, he poured forth enthusiastic eloquence, and then changed quickly to reasoning or wit. His transitions from one thought and feeling, or from one subject and tone to another, were so frequent and rapid, as to surprise, and sometimes to bewilder persons of slow intellect; but always to entertain and delight those of quick capacity. . . .

'His openness in conversation went too far, almost to imprudence, exposing him not only to be misrepresented, but to be misunderstood. . . . Whenever he perceived in any of his friends, or in one of his children, an error of mind, or fault of character, dangerous to their happiness; or when he saw good opportunity of doing them service, by apposite and strong remark or eloquent appeal in conversation, he pursued his object with all the boldness of truth, and with all the warmth of affection. . . .

'I will not deny, what I have heard from some whose truth and sense I cannot question, that his manner, somewhat unusual, of *drawing people out*, however kindly intended, often abashed the timid, and alarmed the cautious; but, in the judgments to be formed of the understandings of all with whom

he conversed, he was uncommonly indulgent. He
allowed for the prejudices or for the deficiencies of
education ; and he foresaw, with the prophetic eye
of benevolence, what the understanding or character
might become if certain improvements were effected.
In discerning genius or abilities of any kind, his
penetration was so quick and just that it seemed
as if he possessed some mental divining-rod re-
vealing to him hidden veins of talent, and giving
him the power of discovering mines of intellectual
wealth, which lay unsuspected even by the possessor.

'To young persons his manner was most kind and
encouraging. I have been gratified by the assurance
that many have owed to the instruction and encouragement received from him in casual conversation
their first hopes of themselves, their resolution to
improve, and a happy change in the colour and
fortune of their future lives. . . . Time mellowed
but did not impair his vivacity ; so that seeming
less connected with high animal spirits, it acquired
more the character of intellectual energy. Still in
age, as in youth, he never needed the stimulus of
convivial company, or of new auditors ; his spirits
and conversation were always more delightful in his
own family and in everyday life than in company,
even the most literary or distinguished.'

The relations between Edgeworth and his daughter

Maria were peculiarly close, and she gratefully acknowledges how much she owed to his suggestions and criticisms. He did not share his friend Mr. Day's objections to literary ladies, and was a great admirer of Mrs. Barbauld's writings :—

'Ever the true friend and champion of female literature, and zealous for the honour of the female sex, he rejoiced with all the enthusiasm of a warm heart when he found, as he now did, female genius guided by feminine discretion. He exulted in every instance of literary celebrity, supported by the amiable and respectable virtues of private life ; proving by example that the cultivation of female talents does not unfit women for their domestic duties and situation in society.'

When Maria began to write she always told her father her rough plan, and he, 'with the instinct of a good critic, used to fix immediately upon that which would best answer the purpose.—" *Sketch that and show it to me.*"—These words' (she adds), 'from the experience of his sagacity, never failed to inspire me with hopes of success. It was then sketched. Sometimes, when I was fond of a particular part, I use to dilate on it in the sketch ; but to this he always objected—" I don't want any of your painting—none of your drapery !—I can imagine all that—let me see the bare skeleton." . . .

'After a sketch had his approbation, he would not see the filling it up till it had been worked upon for a week or a fortnight, or till the first thirty or forty pages were written; then they were read to him; and if he thought them going on tolerably well, the pleasure in his eyes, the approving sound of his voice, even without the praise he so warmly bestowed, were sufficient and delightful excitements to "go on and finish." When he thought that there was spirit in what was written, but that it required, as it often did, great correction, he would say, "Leave that to me; it is my business to *cut* and correct—yours to write on." His skill in *cutting*, his decision in criticism, was peculiarly useful to me. His ready invention and infinite resource, when I had run myself into difficulties or absurdities, never failed to extricate me at my utmost need. . . .

'Independently of all the advantages, which I as an individual received from my father's constant course of literary instruction, this was of considerable utility in another and less selfish point of view. My father called upon all the family to hear and judge of all we were writing. The taste for literature, and for judging of literary composition, was by this means formed and exercised in a large family, including a succession of nine or ten children, who grew up during the course of these twenty-five years. Stories of children exercised the judgment of children, and so on in proportion to their respective ages, all giving their opinions, and trying their powers of criticism fearlessly and freely. . . .

' He would sometimes advise me to lay by what was done for several months, and turn my mind to something else, that we might look back at it afterwards with fresh eyes. . . .

' I may mention, because it leads to a general principle of criticism, that, in many cases, the attempt to join truth and fiction did not succeed : for instance, Mr. Day's educating Sabrina for his wife suggested the story of Virginia and Clarence Hervey in " Belinda." But to avoid representing the real character of Mr. Day, which I did not think it right to draw, I used the incident with fictitious characters, which I made as unlike the real persons as I possibly could. My father observed to me afterwards that, in this and other instances, the very *circumstances* that were taken from real life are those that have been objected to as improbable or impossible ; for this, as he showed me, there are good and sufficient reasons. In the first place, anxiety to avoid drawing the *characters* that were to be blameable or ridiculous from any individuals in real life, led me to apply whatever *circumstances* were taken from reality to characters quite different from those to whom the facts had occurred ; and consequently, when so applied, they were unsuitable and improbable: besides, as my father remarked the circumstances which in real life fix the attention, because they are out of the common course of events, are for this very reason unfit for the moral purposes, as well as for the dramatic effect of fiction. The interest we take in hearing an uncommon fact often depends on our belief in its truth. Introduce it into fiction, and this interest ceases, the reader stops to question the truth or probability of the narrative, the illusion and the dramatic effect are destroyed ; and as to the moral, no safe conclusion for conduct can be drawn from any circumstances which have not frequently happened, and which are not likely often to recur. In proportion as events are extraordinary, they are useless or unsafe as foundations for pruden- tial reasoning.

' Besides all this, there are usually some small con- current circumstances connected with extraordinary facts, which we like and admit as evidences of the truth, but which the rules of composition and taste forbid the introducing into fiction ; so that the writer is reduced to the difficulty either of omitting the evidence on which the belief of reality rests, or of introducing what may be contrary to good taste, incongruous, out of proportion to the rest of the story, delaying its progress or destructive of its unity. In short, it is dangerous to put a patch of truth into a fiction, for the truth is too strong for the fiction, and on all sides pulls it asunder.'

To live with Edgeworth must have been to enjoy a constant mental stimulus; he could not bear his companions to use words without attaching ideas to them; he did not want talk to consist of a fluent utterance of second-hand thoughts, but always encouraged the expression of genuine opinion.

To show how willing Edgeworth was to help a child in understanding a word which was new to it, I will quote from one of his letters to Maria: 'Give my love to little F——, and tell her that I had not time to explain a section to her. I therefore beg that, with as little explanation as possible, you will bisect a lemon before her, and point out the appearance of the rind, of the cavities, and seeds; and afterwards, at your leisure, get a small cylinder of wood turned for her, and cut it into a transverse section and into a longitudinal section.'

It is curious to note the difference in tone which there is between the children's books written by him and Maria and those of the second half of the nineteenth century. Our duty to our neighbour is the Edgeworth watchword, while our duty to God is the

watchword of Miss Yonge and her school of writers.
The swing of the pendulum is constantly passing
from morality to religion and back again, because
both are required for the perfect life.

Among the experiments which Edgeworth made in
the management of his children was that : ' Formerly '
(Maria writes) ' from having observed how apt children
are to dispute and quarrel when they are left much
together, and from fear of the strong becoming tyrants,
and the weak slaves, it had been thought prudent
to separate them a good deal. It was believed that
they would consequently grow fonder of each other's
company, and that they would enjoy it more as they
grew more reasonable, from not having the recollection of anything disagreeable in each other's tempers.
But my father became thoroughly convinced that
the separation of children in a family may lead to
evils greater than any partial good that can result
from it. The attempt may induce artifice and dis-
obedience on the part of the children ; the separation
can scarcely be effected ; and, if it were effected,
would tend to make the children miserable. He saw
that their little quarrels, and the crossings of their
tempers and fancies, are nothing in comparison with
the inestimable blessings of that fondness, that family
affection which grows up among children, who have
with each other an early and constant community of

pleasures and pains. Separation as a punishment, as a just consequence of children's quarrelling, and as the best means of preventing their disputes, he always found useful. But, except in extreme cases, he had rarely recourse to it, and such seldom occurred. . . . The greatest change, which twenty years further experience made in his practice and opinions in education, was to lessen rather than to increase regulations and restrictions. He saw that, where there is liberty of action, one thing balances another ; that nice calculations lead to false results in practice, because we cannot command all the necesssary circumstances of the data. . . .

'For many years of his life he had, I think, been under one important mistake, in his expectations relative to the conduct of his fellow-creatures, and of the effects of cultivating the human understanding. He had believed that, if rational creatures could be made clearly to see and understand that virtue will render them happy, and vice will render them miserable, either in this world or in the next, they would afterwards, in consequence of this conviction, follow virtue, and avoid vice. . . .

'Hence, both as to national and domestic education, he formerly dwelt principally upon the cultivation of the understanding, meaning chiefly the reasoning faculty as applied to the conduct. But to see the

best, and to follow it, are not, alas! necessary consequences of each other. Resolution is often wanting
where conviction is perfect.—Resolution is most
necessary to all our active, and habit most essential
to all our passive virtues. Probably nine times out
of ten the instances of imprudent or vicious conduct
arise, not from want of knowledge of good and evil,
or from want of conviction that the one leads to
happiness, and the other to misery; but from actual
deficiency in the strength of resolution, deficiency
arising from want of early training in the habit of
self-control.'

Maria adds: 'The silence which has been observed
in *Practical Education* on the subject of religion has
been misunderstood by some, and misrepresented by
others. . . . To those who, with upright and benevo-
lent intentions, from a sense of public duty, and in a
spirit of Christian charity, made remonstrances on
this subject, he thought it due to give all the explanation in his power;' and he writes: 'The authors
continue to preserve the silence upon this subject,
which they before thought prudent; but they *dis-
avow, in explicit terms, the design of laying down a
system of education founded upon morality, exclusive of
religion*. . . . We most earnestly deprecate the impu-
tation of disregarding religion in Education. . . . We
are convinced that religious obligation is indispensably

*necessary in the education of all descriptions of people
in every part of the world.*

'We dread fanaticism and intolerance, whilst we
wish to hold religion in a higher point of view than
as a subject of seclusive possession, or of outward
exhibition. To introduce the awful ideas of God's
superintendence upon puerile occasions, we decline.
. . . I hope I shall obtain the justice due to me on
the subject, and that it will appear that I *consider
religion, in the large sense of the word, to be the only
certain bond of society.*

'You have turned back our thoughts to this most
important subject (education), upon which, *next to a
universal reverence for religion*, we believe the happiness of mankind to depend.' Maria adds: 'I have
often been witness of the care with which he explained
the nature and enforced the observance of that great
bond of civil society, which rests upon religion. The
solemnity of the manner in which he administered
an oath can never leave my memory; and I have
seen the salutary effect this produced on the minds
of those of the lower Irish, who are supposed to be
the least susceptible of such impressions. But it was
not on the terrors of religion he chiefly dwelt. No
man could be more sensible than he was of the
consolatory, fortifying influence of the Christian
religion in sustaining the mind in adversity, poverty,

and age. No man knew better its power to carry hope and peace in the hour of death to the penitent criminal. When from party bigotry it has happened that a priest has been denied admittance to the condemned criminal, my father has gone to the county gaol to soothe the sufferer's mind, and to receive that confession on which, to the poor Catholic's belief, his salvation depended. . . . Nor did he ever weaken in any heart in which it ever existed that which he considered as the greatest blessing that a human creature can enjoy—firm religious faith and hope.'

The following extract from a letter written to the Roman Catholics of the County of Longford will show that Edgeworth was no bigoted Protestant, but was in advance of his time in the broad views he took of religious liberty: ' Ever since I have taken any part in the politics of Ireland, I have uniformly thought that there should be no civil distinctions between its inhabitants upon account of their religious opinions. I concurred with a great character at the national convention, in endeavouring to persuade our Roman Catholic brethren to take a decided part in favour of parliamentary reform. They declined it ; and it then became absurd and dangerous for individuals to demand rights in the name of a class of citizens who would not avow their claim to them. . . . I wish . . . to declare myself in favour of a full participation of rights amongst every denomination of men in Ireland ; and if I can, by my personal interference at any public meeting of our county, serve your cause, I shall think it my duty to attend.'

CHAPTER VII

DURING Edgeworth's stay in England in 1792 and 1793 he paid frequent visits to London, and he used to describe to his children a curious meeting which he had in a coffee-house with an old acquaintance whom he had not seen for thirty years: ' He observed a gentleman eyeing him with much attention, who at last exclaimed, "It is he. Certainly, sir, you are Mr. Edgeworth?"

' " I am, sir."

' " Gentlemen," said the · stranger, with much importance, addressing himself to several people who were near him, 'here is the best dancer in England, and a man to whom I am under infinite obligations; for I owe to him the foundation of my fortune. Mr. Edgeworth and I were scholars of the famous Aldridge; and once when we practised together, Mr. Edgeworth excelled me so much, that I sat down upon the ground, and burst out a-crying; he could actually complete an *entrechat* of ten distinct beats, which I could not accomplish! However, I was well

consoled by him ; for he invented, for Aldridge's
benefit, *The Tambourine Dance,* which had uncommon
success. The dresses were Chinese. Twelve assist-
ants held small drums furnished with bells ; these
were struck in the air by the dancer's feet when held
as high as their arms could reach. This Aldridge
performed, and *improved* upon by stretching his legs
asunder, so as to strike two drums at the same time.
Those not being the days of elegant dancing, I afterwards," continued the stranger, "exhibited at Paris the
tambourine dance, to so much advantage, that I made
fifteen hundred pounds by it."

'The person who made this singular address and
eulogium was the celebrated dancer, Mr. Slingsby.
His testimony proves that my father did not overrate
his powers as a dancer ; but it was not to boast of a
frivolous excellence that he told this anecdote to his
children ; it was to express his satisfaction at having,
after the first effervescence of boyish spirits had
subsided, cultivated his understanding, turned his
inventive powers to useful objects, and chosen as the
companions of his maturer years men of the first
order of intellect.'

He also took the opportunity while in England of
visiting his scientific friends—Watt, Darwin, Keir,
and Wedgwood ; and it was now that his friendship began with Mr. William Strutt of Derby,

with whom he became acquainted by means of Mr. Darwin.

It was about this time that he lost his old friend Lord Longford. Maria says of him: 'His services in the British navy, and his character as an Irish senator, have been fully appreciated by the public. His value in private life, and as a friend, can be justly estimated only by those who have seen and felt how strongly his example and opinions have, for a long course of years, continued to influence his family, and all who had the honour of his friendship. The permanence of this influence after death is a stronger proof of the sincerity of the esteem and admiration felt for the character of the individual than any which can be given during his lifetime. I can bear witness that, in one instance, it never ceased to operate. I know that on every important occasion of my father's life, where he was called upon to judge or act, long after Lord Longford was no more, his example and opinions seemed constantly present to him; he delighted in the recollection of instances of his friend's sound judgment, honour, and generosity; these he applied in his own conduct, and held up to the emulation of his children.'

Doubtless Edgeworth felt, as Charles Lamb expresses it: 'Deaths overset one, and put one out long after the recent grief. Two or three have died within the last two twelvemonths, and so many parts of me have been numbed. One sees a picture, reads an anecdote, starts a casual fancy, and thinks to tell of it to this person in preference to every other ; the person is gone whom it would have peculiarly suited. It won't do for another. Every departure destroys a class of sympathies. There's Captain Burney gone ! What fun has whist now? What matters it what you lead if you can no longer fancy him looking over you ? One never hears anything but the image of the particular person occurs with whom alone almost you would care to share the intelligence. Thus one distributes oneself about, and now for so many parts of me I have lost the market.'

The departure of Edgeworth and his family from Clifton in the autumn of 1793 was hastened by the news that disturbances were breaking out in Ireland. Dr. Beddoes of Clifton, who was courting Edgeworth's daughter Anna, had to console himself with the permission to follow her to Ireland in the spring, where they were married at Edgeworth Town in April 1794.

It was not till the autumn of 1794 that the disturbances in Ireland became alarming ; and in a letter to Dr. Darwin, Edgeworth writes : ' Just recovering from the alarm occasioned by a sudden irruption of defenders into this neighbourhood, *and* from the business of a county meeting, *and* the glory of commanding a squadron of horse, *and* from the exertion requisite to treat with proper indifference an anonymous letter sent by persons who have sworn to assassinate me ; I received the peaceful philosophy of *Zoonomia* ; and though it has been in my hands not many minutes, I found much to delight and instruct me. . . .

'We were lately in a sad state here—the *sans culottes* (literally so) took a very effectual way of obtaining power ; they robbed of arms all the houses in the country, thus arming themselves and disarming their opponents. By *waking* the bodies of their friends, the human corpse not only becomes familiar to the *sans culottes* of Ireland, but is associated with pleasure in their minds by the festivity of these nocturnal orgies. An insurrection of such people, who have been much oppressed, must be infinitely more horrid than anything that has happened in France ; for no hired executioners need be sought from the prisons or the galleys. And yet the people here are altogether better than in England. . . . The peasants, though cruel, are generally docile, and of the strongest powers, both of body and mind.

'A good government may make this a great country, because the raw material is good and simple. In England, to make a *carte-blanche* fit to receive a proper impression, you must grind down all the old rags to purify them.'

His daughter adds: 'The disturbances in the county of Longford were quieted for a time by the military; but again in the autumn of the ensuing year (September 1796), rumours of an invasion prevailed, and spread with redoubled force through Ireland, disturbing commerce, and alarming all ranks of well-disposed subjects.'

G

CHAPTER VIII

IT was in 1797 that sorrow again visited the happy circle at Edgeworth Town, and Edgeworth wrote thus of his wife to Dr. Darwin : 'She declines rapidly. But her mind suffers as little as possible. I am convinced from all that I have seen, that *good sense* diminishes all the evils of life, and alleviates even the inevitable pain of declining health. By good sense, I mean that habit of the understanding which employs itself in forming just estimates of every object that lies before it, and in regulating the temper and conduct. Mrs. Edgeworth, ever since I knew her, has carefully improved and cultivated this faculty ; and I do not think I ever saw any person extract more good, and suffer less evil, than she has, from the events of life. . . .'

Mrs. Edgeworth died in the autumn of the year 1797. Maria adds : ' I have heard my father say, that during the seventeen years of his marriage with this lady, he never once saw her out of temper, and never received from her an unkind word or an angry look.'

Edgeworth paid the same compliment to his third wife which he had done to his second—he quickly replaced her. His fourth wife was the daughter of Dr. Beaufort, a highly cultivated man, whose family were great friends of Mrs. Ruxton, Edgeworth's sister. Edgeworth wrote a long letter about scientific matters to Darwin, and kept his most important news to the last: 'I am going to be married to a young lady of small fortune and large accomplishments,—compared with my age, much youth (not quite thirty), and more prudence—some beauty, more sense—uncommon talents, more uncommon temper,—liked by my family, loved by me. If I can say all this three years hence, shall not I have been a fortunate, not to say a wise man?'

Maria adds: 'A few days after the preceding letter was written, we heard that a conspiracy had been discovered in Dublin, that the city was under arms, and its inhabitants in the greatest terror. Dr. Beaufort and his family were there; my father, who was at Edgeworth Town, set out immediately to join them.

'On his way he met an intimate friend of his; one stage they travelled together, and a singular conversation passed. This friend, who as yet knew nothing of my father's intentions, began to speak of the marriage of some other person, and to exclaim against the folly and imprudence of any man's marrying in such disturbed times. "No man of honour, sense or feeling, would incumber himself with a wife at such a time!" My father urged that this was just the time when a man of honour, sense, or feeling would wish, if he loved a woman, to unite his fate with hers, to acquire the right of being her protector.

'The conversation dropped there. But presently they talked of public affairs — of the important measure expected to be proposed, of a union between England and Ireland—of what would probably be said and done in the next session of Parliament: my father, foreseeing that this important national question would probably come on, had just obtained a seat in Parliament. His friend, not knowing or recollecting this, began to speak of the imprudence of commencing a political career late in life.

' "No man, you know," said he, "but a fool, would venture to make a first speech in Parliament, or to marry, after he was fifty."

'My father laughed, and surrendering all title to wisdom, declared that, though he was past fifty, he was actually going in a few days, as he hoped, to be married, and in a few months would probably make his "first speech in Parliament."

'He found Dublin as it had been described to him

under arms, in dreadful expectation. The timely apprehension of the heads of the conspiracy at this crisis prevented a revolution, and saved the capital. But the danger for the country seemed by no means over,—insurrections, which were to have been general and simultaneous, broke out in different parts of the kingdom. The confessions of a conspirator, who had turned informer, and the papers seized and published, proved that there existed in the country a deep and widely spread spirit of rebellion. . . .

'Instead of delaying his marriage, which some would have advised, my father urged for an immediate day. On the 31st of May he was married to Miss Beaufort, by her brother, the Rev. William Beaufort, at St. Anne's Church in Dublin. They came down to Edgeworth Town immediately, through a part of the country that was in actual insurrection. Late in the evening they arrived safe at home, and my father presented his bride to his expecting, anxious family.

'Of her first entrance and appearance that evening I can recollect only the general impression, that it was quite natural, without effort or pretension. The chief thing remarkable was, that she, of whom we were all thinking so much, seemed to think so little of herself. . . .

'The sisters of the late Mrs. Edgeworth, those

excellent aunts (Mrs. Mary and Charlotte Sneyd), instead of returning to their English friends and relations,
remained at Edgeworth Town. This was an auspicious
omen to the common people in our neighbourhood,
by whom they were universally beloved—it spoke
well, they said, for the *new* lady.   In his own family,
the union and happiness she would secure were soon
felt, but her superior qualities, her accurate knowledge, judgment, and abilities, in decision and in
action, appeared only as occasions arose and called
for them.   She was found always equal to the occasion, and superior to the expectation.'

Maria had not at first been in favour of her father's
marrying Miss Beaufort, but she soon changed her
opinion after becoming intimate with her, and writing
of her father's choice of a wife says : ' He did not late
in life marry merely to please his own fancy, but he
chose a companion suited to himself, and a mother
fit for his family.   This, of all the blessings we owe
to him, has proved the greatest.'

The family at Edgeworth Town passed the summer
quietly and happily, but (Maria continues) ' towards
the autumn of the year 1798, this country became in
such a state that the necessity of resorting to the
sword seemed imminent.   Even in the county of
Longford, which had so long remained quiet, alarming symptoms appeared, not immediately in our

neighbourhood, but within six or seven miles of us, near Granard. The people were leagued in secret rebellion, and waited only for the expected arrival of the French army to break out. In the adjacent counties military law had been proclaimed, and our village was within a mile of the bounds of the disturbed county of Westmeath. Though his own tenantry, and all in whom he put trust, were as quiet, and, as far as he could judge, as well-disposed as ever, yet my father was aware, from information of too good authority to be doubted, that there were disaffected persons in the vicinity.

'Numbers held themselves in abeyance, not so much from disloyalty, as from fear that they should be ultimately the conquered party. Those who were really and actually engaged, and in communication with the rebels and with the foreign enemy, were so secret and cunning that no proofs could be obtained against them.

'One instance may be given. A Mr. Pallas, who lived at Growse Hall, lately received information that a certain offender was to be found in a lone house, which was described to him. He took a party of men with him in the night, and he got to the house very early in the morning. It was scarcely light. The soldiers searched, but no man was to be found. Mr. Pallas ordered them to search again,

for that he was certain the man was in the house ;
they searched again, but in vain ; they gave up the
point, and were preparing to mount their horses,
when one man, who had stayed a little behind his
companions, saw, or thought he saw, something
move at the end of the garden behind the house.
He looked, and beheld a man's arm come out of
the ground : he ran to the spot and called to his
companions ; but the arm disappeared ; they searched,
but nothing was to be seen ; and though the soldier
still persisted in his story, he was not believed.
" Come," cries one of the party, " don't waste your
time here looking for an apparition among these
cabbage-stalks—go back once more to the house ! "
They went to the house, and lo ! there stood the
man they were in search of in the middle of the
kitchen.

' Upon examination it was found that from his
garden to his house there had been practised a secret
passage underground: a large meal-chest in the kitchen had a false bottom, which lifted up and down at
pleasure, to let him into his subterraneous dwelling.

' Whenever he expected the house to be searched,
down he went ; the moment the search was over,
up he came ; and had practised this with success,
till he grew rash, and returned one moment too
soon. . . .

'Previous to this time, the principal gentry in the county had raised corps of yeomanry; but my father had delayed doing so, because, as long as the civil authority had been sufficient, he was unwilling to resort to military interference, or to the ultimate law of force, of the abuse of which he had seen too many recent examples. However, it now became necessary, even for the sake of justice to his own tenantry, that they should be put upon a footing with others, have equal security of protection, and an opportunity of evincing their loyal dispositions. He raised a corps of infantry, into which he admitted Catholics as well as Protestants. This was so un-usual, and thought to be so hazardous a degree of liberality, that by some of an opposite party it was attributed to the worst motives. Many who wished him well came privately to let him know of the odium to which he exposed himself.

'The corps of Edgeworth Town infantry was raised, but the arms were, by some mistake of the ordnance-officer, delayed. The anxiety for their arrival was extreme, for every day and every hour the French were expected to land.

'The alarm was now so general that many sent their families out of the country. My father was still in hopes that we might safely remain. At the first appearance of disturbance in Ireland he had offered to carry his sisters-in-law, the Mrs. Sneyd, to their friends in England, but this offer they refused. Of the domestics, three men were English and Protestant, two Irish and Catholic; the women were all Irish and Catholic excepting the housekeeper, an Englishwoman, who had lived with us many years. There were no dissensions or suspicions between the Catholics and the Protestants in the family; and the English servants did not desire to quit us at this crisis.

'At last came the dreaded news. The French, who landed at Killala, were, as we learned, on their march towards Longford. The touch of Ithuriel's spear could not have been more sudden or effectual than the arrival of this intelligence in showing people in their real forms. In some faces joy struggled for a moment with feigned sorrow, and then, encouraged by sympathy, yielded to the *natural* expression. Still my father had no reason to distrust those in whom he had placed confidence; his tenants were steady; he saw no change in any of the men of his corps, though they were in the most perilous situation, having rendered themselves obnoxious to the rebels and invaders by becoming yeomen, and yet standing without means of resistance or defence, their arms not having arrived.

'The evening of the day when the news of the

success and approach of the French came to Edgeworth Town all seemed quiet; but early next morning,
September 4th, a report reached us that the rebels
were *up* in arms within a mile of the village, pouring
in from the county of Westmeath hundreds strong.
. . . This much being certain, that men armed with
pikes were assembled, my father sent off an express
to the next garrison town (Longford) requesting the
commanding officer to send him assistance for the
defence of this place. He desired us to be prepared
to set out at a moment's warning. We were under
this uncertainty, when an escort with an ammunition
cart passed through the village on its way to Longford. It contained several barrels of powder, intended
to blow up the bridges, and to stop the progress of
the enemy. One of the officers of the party rode up
to our house and offered to let us have the advantage
of his escort. But, after a few minutes' deliberation,
this friendly proposal was declined : my father determined that he would not stir till he knew whether he
could have assistance ; and as it did not appear as
yet absolutely necessary that we should go, we stayed
—fortunately for us.

'About a quarter of an hour after the officer and
the escort had departed, we, who were all assembled
in the portico of the house, heard a report like a loud
clap of thunder. The doors and windows shook with

some violent concussion: a few minutes afterwards
the officer galloped into the yard, and threw himself
off his horse into my father's arms almost senseless.
The ammunition cart had blown up, one of the officers
had been severely wounded, and the horses and the
man leading them killed ; the wounded officer was
at a farmhouse on the Longford road, at about two
miles' distance. The fear of the rebels was now
suspended in concern for this accident ; Mrs. Edgeworth went immediately to give her assistance ; she
left her carriage for the use of the wounded gentleman,
and rode back. At the entrance of the village she
was stopped by a gentleman in great terror, who,
taking hold of the bridle of her horse, begged her not
to attempt to go farther, assuring her that the rebels
were coming into the town. But she answered that
she must and would return to her family. She rode
on, and found us waiting anxiously for her. No
assistance could be afforded from Longford ; the
rebels were reassembling, and advancing towards
the village ; and there was no alternative but to
leave our house as fast as possible. One of our
carriages having been left with the wounded officer,
we had but one at this moment for our whole family,
eleven in number. No mode of conveyance could be
had for some of our female servants ; our faithful
English housekeeper offered to stay till the return of

the carriage, which had been left with the officer ; and as we could not carry her, we were obliged, most reluctantly, to leave her behind to follow, as we hoped, immediately.   As we passed through the village we heard nothing but the entreaties, lamentations, and objurations of those who could not procure the means of carrying off their goods or their families ; most painful when we could give no assistance.

' Next to the safety of his own family, my father's greatest anxiety was for his defenceless corps. No men could behave better than they did at this first moment of trial.   Not one absented himself, though many, living at a distance, might, if they had been so inclined, have found plausible excuses for non-appearance.

' He ordered them to march to Longford.   The idea of going to Longford could not be agreeable to many of them, who were Catholics.   There was no reluctance shown, however, by the Catholics of this corps to go among those who called themselves Orangemen.

' We expected every instant to hear the shout of the rebels entering Edgeworth Town.   When we had got about half-a-mile out of the village, my father suddenly recollected that he had left on his table a paper containing a list of his corps, and that, if this should come into the hands of the rebels, it might be of dangerous consequence to his men ; it would serve

to point out their houses for pillage, and their families
for destruction. He turned his horse instantly and
galloped back for it. The time of his absence
appeared immeasurably long, but he returned safely
after having destroyed the dangerous paper.

'Longford was crowded with yeomanry of various
corps, and with the inhabitants of the neighbourhood,
who had flocked thither for protection. With great
difficulty the poor Edgeworth Town infantry found
lodgings. We were cordially received by the landlady of a good inn. Though her house was, as she
said, fuller than it could hold, as she was an old friend
of my father's, she did contrive to give us two rooms,
in which we eleven were thankful to find ourselves.
All our concern now was for those we had left behind.
We heard nothing of our housekeeper all night, and
were exceedingly alarmed ; but early the next morning, to our great joy, she arrived. She told us that,
after we had left her, she waited hour after hour for
the carriage ; she could hear nothing of it, as it had
gone to Longford with the wounded officer. Towards
evening, a large body of rebels entered the village ;
she heard them at the gate, and expected that they
would have broken in the next instant ; but one, who
seemed to be a leader, with a pike in his hand, set
his back against the gate, and swore that, if he was
to die for it the next minute, he would have the life

of the first man who should open that gate or set enemy's foot withinside of that place. He said the housekeeper, who was left in it, was a good gentle-woman, and had done him a service, *though she did not know him, nor he her.* He had never seen her face, but she had, the year before, lent his wife, when in distress, sixteen shillings, the rent of flax-ground, and he would stand her friend now.

'He kept back the mob: they agreed to send him to the house with a deputation of six, *to know the truth*, and to ask for arms. The six men went to the back door and summoned the housekeeper; one of them pointed his blunderbuss at her, and told her that she must fetch all the arms in the house; she said she had none. Her champion asked her to say if she remembered him. "No," to her knowledge she had never seen his face. He asked if she remembered having lent a woman money to pay her rent of flax-ground the year before. "Yes," she remembered that, and named the woman, the time, and the sum. His companions were thus satisfied of the truth of what he had asserted. He bid her not to be *frighted*, for that no harm should happen to her, nor any be-longing to her; not a soul should get leave to go into her master's house; not a twig should be touched, nor a leaf harmed. His companions huzzaed and went off. Afterwards, as she was told, he mounted guard at the gate during the whole time the rebels were in the town.

'When the carriage at last returned, it was stopped by the rebels, who filled the street; they held their pikes to the horses and to the coachman's breast, accusing him of being an Orangeman, because, as they said, he wore the orange colours (our livery being yellow and brown). A painter, a friend of ours, who had been that day at our house, copying some old family portraits, happened to be in the street at that instant, and called out to the mob, "Gentlemen, it is yellow! Gentlemen, it is not orange!" In consequence of this happy distinction they let go the coachman; and the same man who had mounted guard at the gate, came up with his friends, rescued the carriage, and surrounding the coachman with their pikes brought him safely into the yard. The pole of the carriage having been broken in the first onset, the housekeeper could not leave Edgeworth Town till morning. She passed the night in walking up and down, listening and watching, but the rebels returned no more, and thus our house was saved by the gratitude of a single individual.

'We had scarcely time to rejoice in the escape of our housekeeper and safety of our house, when we found that new dangers arose even from this escape. The house being saved created jealousy and suspicion

in the minds of many, who at this time saw everything through the mist of party prejudice. The
dislike to my father's corps appeared every hour
more strong. He saw the consequences that might
arise from the slightest breaking out of quarrel. It
was not possible for him to send his men, unarmed
as they still were, to their homes, lest they should
be destroyed by the rebels; yet the officers of the
other corps wished to have them sent out of the
town, and to this effect joined in a memorial to
government. Some of these officers disliked my
father, from differences of electioneering interests;
others, from his not having kept up an acquaintance
with them; and others, not knowing him in the
least, were misled by party reports and misrepre-
sentations.

'These petty dissensions were, however, at one
moment suspended and forgotten in a general sense
of danger. An express arrived late one night with
the news that the French, who were rapidly advancing, were within a few miles of the town of
Longford. A panic seized the people. There
were in the town eighty of the carabineers and
two corps of yeomanry, but it was proposed to
evacuate the garrison. My father strongly opposed
this measure, and undertook, with fifty men, if arms
and ammunition were supplied, to defend the gaol of

Longford, where there was a strong pass, at which
the enemy might be stopped. He urged that a
stand might be made there till the King's army
should come up. The offer was gladly accepted—
men, arms, and ammunition, all he could want or
desire, were placed at his disposal. He slept that
night in the gaol, with everything prepared for its
defence; but the next morning fresh news came,
that the French had turned off from the Longford
Road, and were going towards Granard; of this,
however, there was no certainty. My father, by the
desire of the commanding officer, rode out to recon-
noitre, and my brother went to the top of the court-
house with a telescope for the same purpose. We
(Mrs. Edgeworth, my aunts, my sisters, and myself)
were waiting to hear the result in one of the upper
sitting-rooms of the inn, which fronted the street.
We heard a loud shout, and going to the window,
we saw the people throwing up their hats, and heard
huzzas. An express had arrived with news that
the French and the rebels had been beaten; that
General Lake had come up with them at a place
called Ballynamuck, near Granard; that 1500 rebels
and French were killed, and that the French generals
and officers were prisoners.

'We were impatient for my father, when we heard
this joyful news; he had not yet returned, and we

looked out of the window in hopes of seeing him; but we could see only a great number of people of the town shaking hands with each other. This lasted a few minutes, and then the crowd gathered in silence round one man, who spoke with angry vehemence and gesticulation, stamping, and frequently wiping his forehead. We thought he was a mountebank haranguing the populace, till we saw that he wore a uniform. Listening with curiosity to hear what he was saying, we observed that he looked up towards us, and we thought we heard him pronounce the names of my father and brother in tones of insult. We could scarcely believe what we heard him say. Pointing up to the top of the court-house, he exclaimed, " *That* young Edgeworth ought to be dragged down from the top of that house."

'Our housekeeper burst into the room, so much terrified she could hardly speak.

'" My master, ma'am !—it is all against my master. The mob say they will tear him to pieces, if they catch hold of him. They say he 's a traitor, that he illuminated the gaol to deliver it up to the French."

' No words can give an idea of our astonishment. " Illuminated ! " What could be meant by the gaol being illuminated ? My father had literally but two farthing candles, by the light of which he had been reading the newspaper late the preceding night. These, however, were said to be signals for the enemy. The absurdity of the whole was so glaring that we could scarcely conceive the danger to be real, but our pale landlady's fears were urgent; she dreaded that her house should be pulled down.

' We wrote immediately to the commanding officer, informing him of what we had heard, and requesting his advice and assistance. He came to us, and recommended that we should send a messenger to warn Mr. Edgeworth of his danger, and to request that he would not return to Longford that day. The officer added that, in consequence of the rejoicings for the victory, his men would probably be all drunk in a few hours, and that he could not answer for them. This officer, a captain of yeomanry, was a good-natured but inefficient man, who spoke under considerable nervous agitation, and seemed desirous to do all he could, but not to be able to do anything. We wrote instantly, and with difficulty found a man who undertook to convey the note. It was to be carried to meet him on one road, and Mrs. Edgeworth and I determined to drive out to meet him on the other. We made our way down a back staircase into the inn yard, where the carriage was ready. Several gentlemen spoke to us as we got into the carriage, begging us not to be alarmed:

Mrs. Edgeworth answered that she was more surprised than alarmed. The commanding officer and
the sovereign of Longford walked by the side of
the carriage through the town; and as the mob
believed that we were going away not to return,
we got through without much molestation. We
went a few miles on the road toward Edgeworth
Town, till at a tenant's house we heard that my
father had passed half an hour ago; that he was
riding in company with an officer, supposed to be
of Lord Cornwallis's or General Lake's army; that
they had taken a *short cut*, which led into Longford
by another entrance :—most fortunately, not that at
which an *armed* mob had assembled, expecting the
object of their fury. Seeing him return to the inn
with an officer of the King's army, they imagined,
as we were afterwards told, that he was brought
back a prisoner, and they were satisfied.

'The moment we saw him safe, we laughed at our
own fears, and again doubted the reality of the
danger, more especially as he treated the idea with
the utmost incredulity and scorn.

'Major (now General) Eustace was the officer who
returned with him. He dined with us; everything
appeared quiet. The persons who had taken refuge
at the inn were now gone to their homes, and it
was supposed that, whatever dispositions to riot

had existed, the news of the approach of some of
Lord Cornwallis's suite, or of troops who were to
bring in the French prisoners, would prevent all
probability of disturbance. In the evening the
prisoners arrived at the inn ; a crowd followed them,
but quietly. A sun-burnt, coarse-looking man, in
a huge cocked hat, with a quantity of gold lace on
his clothes, seemed to fix all attention ; he was
pointed out as the French General Homberg, or
Sarrazin. As he dismounted from his horse, he
threw the bridle over its neck, and looked at the
animal as being his only friend.

'We heard my father in the evening ask Major
Eustace to walk with him through the town to the
barrack-yard to evening parade ; and we saw them
go out together without our feeling the slightest
apprehension. We remained at the inn. By this
time Colonel Handfield, Major Cannon, and some
other officers, had arrived, and they were at the inn
at dinner in a parlour on the ground-floor, under our
room. It being hot weather, the windows were
open. Nothing now seemed to be thought of but
rejoicings for the victory. Candles were preparing
for the illumination ; waiters, chambermaids, landlady, were busy scooping turnips and potatoes for
candlesticks, to stand in every pane of every loyal
window.

'In the midst of this preparation, half an hour after my father had left us, we heard a great uproar in the street. At first we thought the shouts were only rejoicings for victory, but as they came nearer we heard screechings and yellings indescribably horrible. A mob had gathered at the gates of the barrack-yard, and joined by many soldiers of the yeomanry on leaving parade, had followed Major Eustace and my father from the barracks. The Major being this evening in coloured clothes, the people no longer knew him to be an officer, nor conceived, as they had done before, that Mr. Edgeworth was his prisoner. The mob had not contented themselves with the horrid yells that they heard, but had been pelting them with hard turf, stones, and brickbats. From one of these my father received a blow on the side of his head, which came with such force as to stagger and almost to stun him ; but he kept himself from falling, knowing that if he once fell he would be trampled under foot. He walked on steadily till he came within a few yards of the inn, when one of the mob seized hold of Major Eustace by the collar. My father seeing the windows of the inn open, called with a loud voice, " Major Eustace is in danger !"

'The officers, who were at dinner, and who till that moment had supposed the noise in the street to be only drunken rejoicings, immediately ran out and rescued Major Eustace and my father. At the sight of British officers and drawn swords, the populace gave way, and dispersed in different directions.

'The preparation for the illumination then went on as if nothing had intervened. All the panes of our windows in the front room were in a blaze of light by the time the mob returned through the street. The night passed without further disturbance.

'As early as we could the next morning we left Longford, and returned homewards, all danger from rebels being now over, and the Rebellion having been terminated by the late battle.

'When we came near Edgeworth Town, we saw many well-known faces at the cabin doors looking out to welcome us. One man, who was digging in his field by the roadside, when he looked up as our horses passed, and saw my father, let fall his spade and clasped his hands; his face, as the morning sun shone upon it, was the strongest picture of joy I ever saw. The village was a melancholy spectacle; windows shattered and doors broken. But though the mischief done was great, there had been little pillage. Within our gates we found all property safe; literally "not a twig touched, nor a leaf harmed." Within the house everything was as we had left it—a map that we had been consulting was still open upon the library table, with pencils, and slips of paper containing the first lessons in arithmetic, in which some of the young people had been engaged the morning we had driven from home ; a pansy, in a glass of water, which one of the children had been copying, was still on the chimney-piece. These trivial circumstances, marking repose and tranquillity, struck us at this moment with an unreasonable sort of surprise, and all that had passed seemed like an incoherent dream. The joy of having my father in safety remained, and gratitude to Heaven for his preservation. These feelings spread inexpressible pleasure over what seemed to be a new sense of existence. Even the most common things appeared delightful ; the green lawn, the still groves, the birds singing, the fresh air, all external nature, and all the goods and conveniences of life, seemed to have wonderfully increased in value from the fear into which we had been put of losing them irrevocably.

'The first thing my father did, the day we came home, was to draw up a memorial to the Lord-Lieutenant, desiring to have a court-martial held on the sergeant who, by haranguing the populace, had raised the mob at Longford ; his next care was to walk through the village, to examine what damage had been done by the rebels, and to order that repairs of all his tenants' houses should be made at his expense. A few days after our return, Government ordered that the arms of the Edgeworth Town infantry should be forwarded by the commanding-officer at Longford. Through the whole of their hard week's trial the corps had, without any exception, behaved perfectly well. It was perhaps more difficult to honest and brave men passively to bear such a trial than any to which they could have been exposed in action.

'When the arms for the corps arrived, my father, in delivering them to the men, thanked them publicly for their conduct, assuring them that he would remember it whenever he should have opportunities of serving them, collectively or individually. In long-after years, as occasions arose, each who continued to deserve it found in him a friend, and felt that he more than fulfilled his promise. . . . Before we quit this subject, it may be useful to record that the French generals who headed this invasion declared they had been completely deceived as to the state of Ireland. They had expected to find the people in open rebellion, or at least, in their own phrase, *organised* for insurrection; but to their dismay they found only ragamuffins, as they called them, who, in joining their standard, did them infinitely more harm than good. It is a pity that the lower Irish could not hear the contemptuous manner in which the French, both officers and soldiers, spoke of them and of their country. The generals described the stratagems which had been practised upon them by their good allies—the same rebels frequently returning with different tones and new stories, to obtain double and treble provisions of arms, ammunition, and uniforms—selling the ammunition for whisky, and running away at the first fire in the day of battle. The French, detesting and despising those by whom they had been thus cheated, pillaged, and deserted, called them beggars, rascals, and savages. They cursed also without scruple their own Directory for sending them, after they had, as they boasted, conquered the world, to be at last beaten on an Irish bog. Officers and soldiers joined in swearing that they would never return to a country where they could find neither bread, wine, nor discipline, and where the people lived on roots, whisky, and lying.'

Maria ends this exciting chapter of the *Memoirs* with these moral reflections : ' At all times it is disadvantageous to those who have the reputation of being men of superior abilities, to seclude themselves from the world. It raises a belief that they despise those with whom they do not associate ; and this supposed contempt creates real aversion. The being accused of pride or singularity may not, perhaps, in the estimation of some lofty spirits and independent characters, appear too great a price to pay for liberty and leisure ; they will care little if they be misunderstood or misrepresented by the vulgar ; they will trust to truth and time to do them justice. This may be all well in ordinary life, and in peaceable days; but in civil commotions the best and the wisest, if he have not made himself publicly known, so as to connect himself with the interests and feelings of his neighbours, will find none to answer for his character if it be attacked, or to warn him of the secret machinations of his enemies ; none who on any sudden emergency will risk their own safety in his defence : he may fall and be trampled upon by numbers, simply because it is nobody's business or pleasure to rally to his aid. Time and reason right his character, and may bring all who have injured, or all who have mistaken him, to repentance and shame, but in the interval he *must* suffer —he *may* perish.'

CHAPTER IX

THE British Government seem to have thought it best at this time to pursue a *laissez faire* policy in Ireland, in order to convince the Irish of their weakness, and to show them that, although a bundle of sticks when loosened allows each stick to be used for beating, and it may therefore be argued that sticks, being meant for fighting, should never be bound in a bundle, yet each single stick may easily get broken. Of course the Government intended to intervene before it was too late, and to suggest to the Irish that it was time to think of a union with their stronger neighbours.

On this subject Maria remarks :—' It is certain that the combinations of the disaffected at home, and the advance of foreign invaders, were not checked till the peril became imminent, and till the purpose of creating universal alarm had been fully effected. As soon as the Commander-in-Chief and the Lord-Lieutenant (at that time joined in the same person) exerted his full military and civil power, the invaders were defeated, and the rebellion was extinguished. The petty magisterial tyrants, who had been worse than vain of their little brief authority, were put down, or rather, being no longer upheld, sank to their original and natural insignificance. The laws returned to their due course; and, with justice, security and tranquillity, were restored.

'My father honestly, not ostentatiously, used his utmost endeavours to obliterate all that could tend to perpetuate ill-will in the country. Among the lower classes in his neighbourhood he endeavoured to discourage that spirit of recrimination and re-taliation which the lower Irish are too prone to cherish, and of which they are proud. "*Revenge is sweet, and I'll have it*," were words which an old beggar-woman was overheard muttering to herself as she tottered along the road. . . .

'The lower Irish are such acute observers that there is no deceiving them as to the state of the real feelings of their superiors. . . .

'It was soon seen by all of those who had any connection with him, that my father was sincere in his disdain of vengeance—of this they had convincing proof in his refusing to listen to the tales of slander, which so many were ready to pour into his ear, against those who had appeared to be his enemies.

'They saw that he determined to have a public trial of the man who had instigated the Longford mob, but *that*, for the sake of justice, and to record what his own conduct had been, he did not seek this trial from any petty motives of personal resentment.

'During the course of the trial, it appeared that the sergeant was a mere ignorant enthusiast, who had been worked up to frenzy by some, more designing than himself. Having accomplished his own object of publicly proving every fact that concerned his own honour and character, my father felt desirous that the poor culprit, who was now ashamed and penitent, should not be punished. The evidence was not pressed against him, and he was acquitted. As they were leaving the court-house my father saw, and spoke in a playful tone to the penitent sergeant, who, among his other weaknesses, happened to be much afraid of ghosts. "Sergeant, I congratulate you," said he, "upon my being alive here before you—I believe you would rather meet me than my ghost!" Then cheering up the man with the assurance of his perfect forgiveness, he passed on.

'The malevolent passions my father always considered as the greatest foes to human felicity—they would not stay in his mind—he was of too good and too happy a nature. He forgot all, but the moral which he drew for his private use from this Longford business. He kept ever afterwards the resolution he had made, to mix more with general society.

'His thoughts were soon called to that most important question, of the Union between England and Ireland, which it was expected would be discussed at the meeting of Parliament.

'It was late in life to begin a political career—imprudently so, had it been with the common views of family advancement or of personal fame ; but his chief hope, in going into Parliament, was to obtain assistance in forwarding the great object of improving the education of the people : he wished also to assist in the discussion of the Union. He was not without a natural desire, which he candidly avowed, to satisfy himself how far he could succeed as a parliamentary speaker, and how far his mind would stand the trial of political competition or the temptations of ambition.

'On the subject of the Union he had not yet been able, in parliamentary phrase, *to make up his mind* : and he went to the House in that state in which so many profess to find themselves, and so few ever really are—anxious to hear the arguments on both sides, and open to be decided by whoever could show him that which was best for his country.

'The debate on the first proposal of the Union was

protracted to an unusual length, and when he rose to
speak, it was late at night, or rather it was early in
the morning—two o'clock—the House had been so
wearied that many of the members were asleep. It
was an inauspicious moment. No person present,
not even the Speaker, who was his intimate friend,
could tell on which side he would vote. Curiosity
was excited : some of the outstretched members were
roused by their neighbours, whose anxiety to know
on which side he would vote prompted them to
encourage him to proceed. This curiosity was kept
alive as he went on ; and when people perceived that
it was not a *set* speech, they became interested. He
stated his doubts, just as they had really occurred,
balancing the arguments as he threw them by turns
into each scale, as they had balanced one another in
his judgment ; so that the doubtful beam nodded from
side to side, while all watched to see when its vibra-
tions would settle. All the time he kept both parties
in good humour, because each expected to have him
their own at last. After stating many arguments in
favour of what appeared to him to be the advantages
of the Union, he gave his vote against it, because, he
said, he had been convinced by what he had heard in
that House this night, that the Union was at this time
decidedly against the wishes of the great majority of
men of sense and property in the nation. He added

that if he should be convinced that the opinion of the country changed at the final discussion of the question, his vote would be in its favour.

'One of the anti-Unionists, who happened not to know my father personally, imagined from his accent, style, and manner of speaking, that he was an Englishman, and accused the Government of having brought a new member over from England, to impose him upon the House, as an impartial country gentleman, who was to make a pretence of liberality by giving a vote against the Union, while, by arguing in its favour, he was to make converts for the measure. Many on the Ministerial bench, who had still hopes that, on a future occasion, Mr. Edgeworth might be *convinced* and brought to vote with them, complimented him highly, declaring that they were completely surprised when they learned how he voted ; for that undoubtedly the best arguments on their side of the question had been produced in his speech. Lord Castlereagh found the measure so much against the sense of the House that he pressed it no further at that time.

'This session my father had the satisfaction of turning the attention of the House to a subject which he considered to be of greater and more permanent importance than the Union, or than any merely political measure could prove to his country, *the education of the people.* By his exertions a select committee was appointed, and they adopted the resolutions drawn up by him. When the report of this committee was brought up to the House, my father spoke at large upon the subject.

'In his speech he said: It was impossible, when moral principles are instilled into the human mind, when people are regularly taught their duty to God and man, that abominable tenets can prevail to the subversion of subordination and society. He would venture to assert, though the power of the sword was great, that the force of education was greater. It was notorious that the writings of one man, Mr. Burke, had changed the opinions of the whole people of England against the French Revolution. . . . If proper books were circulated through the country, and if the public mind was prepared for the reception of their doctrines, it would be impossible to make the ignorance of the people an instrument of national ruin.

'There is, he contended, a fund of goodness in the Irish as well as in the English nature. Did God give different minds to different countries? No, the difference of mind arose from education. It therefore became the duty of Parliament to improve as much as possible the public understanding—for the misfortunes of Ireland were owing not to the heart, but the head : the defect was not from nature, but from want of culture.

' During this session my father spoke again two or three times, on some questions of revenue regulations and excise laws : of little consequence separately considered, but of importance in one respect, in their effect on the morality of the people. He pointed out that nothing could with more certainty tend to increase the crime of perjury than the multiplying custom-house oaths, and what are termed oaths of office. . . . In Ireland the habits of the common people are already too lax with regard to truth. The difference of religion, and the facilities of absolution, present difficulties so formidable to their moral improvement as to require all the counteracting powers of education, example, public opinion, and law. . . . Multiplying oaths injures the revenue, by increasing incalculably the means of evading the very laws and penalties by which it is attempted to bind the subject. Experience proves that this is a danger of no small account to the revenue ; though trifling when compared with the importance of the general effect on national morality, and on the safety and tranquillity of the State, all which must ultimately rest, at all times and in all countries, upon religious sanctions. " It was not," my father observed, " by increasing pains and penalties, or by any severity of punishment, that the observance of laws can be secured ; on the contrary, small but certain punishments, and few but punctually executed laws, are most likely to secure obedience, and to effect public prosperity." '

He writes to Darwin in March 1800 : ' The fatigue of the session was enormous. I am a Unionist, but I vote and speak against the union now proposed to us—as to my reasons, are they not published in the reports of our debates ? It is intended to force this measure down the throats of the Irish, though five-sixths of the nation are against it. Now, though I think such union as would identify the nations, so as that Ireland should be as Yorkshire to Great Britain, would be an excellent thing : yet I also think that the good people of Ireland ought to be *persuaded* of this truth, and not be dragooned into the submission.

' The Minister avows that seventy-two boroughs are to be compensated—*i.e.* bought by the people of Ireland with one million and a half of their own money ; and he makes this legal by a very small majority, made up chiefly by these very borough members. When thirty-eight country members out of sixty-four are against the measure, and *twenty-eight* counties out of *thirty-two* have petitioned against it, this is such abominable corruption that it makes out parliamentary sanction worse than ridiculous.

' I had the honour of offering, for myself, and for a large number of other gentlemen, that, if a minister could by any means win the nation to the measure, and show us even a small preponderance in his favour, we would vote with him.

' So far for politics.   I had a charming opportunity of advancing myself and my family, but I did not think it wise *to quarrel with myself*, and lose my good opinion at my time of life.   What *did* lie in my way for a vote I will not say, but I stated in my place in the House, that I had been offered three thousand guineas for my seat during the few remaining weeks of the session.'

In 1817 he writes :—' The *influence* of the Crown was never so strongly exerted as upon this occasion. It is but justice, however, to Lord Cornwallis and Lord Castlereagh to give it as my opinion, that they *began* this measure with sanguine hopes that they could convince the reasonable part of the community that a cordial union between the two countries would essentially advance the interests of both.   When, however, the ministry found themselves in a minority, and that a spirit of general opposition was rising in the country, a member of the House, who had been long practised in parliamentary intrigues, had the audacity to tell Lord Castlereagh from his place, that "if he did not employ the *usual means of persuasion* on the members of the House, he would fail in his attempt, and that the sooner he set about it the better."

'This advice was followed ; and it is well known what benches were filled with the proselytes that had been made by the *convincing arguments* which had obtained a majority.

'He went in the spring of 1799 to England, and visited his old friends, Mr. Keir, Mr. Watt, Dr. Darwin, and Mr. William Strutt of Derby. In passing through different parts of the country he saw, and delighted in showing us, everything curious and interesting in art and nature. Travelling, he used to say, was from time to time necessary, to change the course of ideas, and to prevent the growth of local prejudices.

'He went to London, and paid his respects to his friend Sir Joseph Banks, attended the meetings of the Royal Society, and met various old acquaintances whom he had formerly known abroad.'

Maria writes :—' In his own account of his earlier life he has never failed to mark the time and manner of the commencement of valuable friendships with the same care and vividness of recollection with which some men mark the date of their obtaining promotion, places, or titles. I follow the example he has set me.

'My father's and Mrs. Edgeworth's families were both numerous, and among such numbers, even granting the dispositions to be excellent and the understandings cultivated, the chances were against their suiting ; but, happily, all the individuals of the two families, though of various talents, ages, and characters, did, from their first acquaintance, coalesce. . . . After he had lost such a friend as Mr. Day . . . who could have dared to hope that he should ever have found another equally deserving to possess his whole confidence and affection ? Yet such a one it pleased God to give him—and to give him in the brother of his wife. And never man felt more strongly grateful for the double blessing. To Captain Beaufort he became as much attached as he had ever been to Lord Longford or to Mr. Day.

'His father-in-law, Dr. Beaufort, was also particularly agreeable to him as a companion, and helpful as a friend.'

Consumption again carried off one of Edgeworth's family : his daughter Elizabeth died at Clifton in August 1800.

The Continent, which had been practically closed for some years to travellers, was open in 1802 at the time of the short peace, and Edgeworth gladly availed himself of the opportunity of mixing in the literary and scientific society in Paris, and of showing

his wife the treasures of the Louvre—treasures increased by the spoil of other countries. The tour
was arranged for the autumn, and Edgeworth was
looking forward to visiting Dr. Darwin on the way,
when he received a letter begun by the doctor, describing his move from Derby to the Priory, a few
miles out of the town, and sending a playful message
to Maria: 'Pray tell the authoress that the water
nymphs of our valley will be happy to assist her next
novel.'

A few lines after, the pen had stopped ; another
hand added the sad news that Dr. Darwin had been
taken suddenly ill with fainting fits : he revived and
spoke, but died that morning. The sudden death of
such an old and valued friend was a great shock to
Edgeworth.

Some months later, his daughter mentions that,
'in passing through England, we went to Derby, and
to the Priory, to which we had been so kindly invited by him who was now no more. The Priory
was all stillness, melancholy, and mourning. It was
a painful visit, yet not without satisfaction ; for my
father's affectionate manner seemed to soothe the
widow and daughters of his friend, who were deeply
sensible of the respect and zealous regard he showed
for Dr. Darwin's memory.'

CHAPTER X

MR. AND MRS. EDGEWORTH, with their daughters
Maria and Charlotte, travelled through the Low
Countries—'a delightful tour,' Maria writes—and at
length reached Paris, where they spent the winter
1802-3. They soon got introductions, through the
Abbé Morellet, into that best circle of society, 'which
was composed of all that remained of the ancient men
of letters, and of the most valuable of the nobility ;
not of those who had accepted of places from Buonaparte, nor yet of those emigrants who have been
wittily and too justly described as returning to
France after the Revolution, *sans avoir rien appris, ou
rien oublié.*' . . . 'We felt,' Maria writes, ' the characteristic charms of Parisian conversation, the polish
and ease which in its best days distinguished it from
that of any other capital.

'During my father's former residence in France, at
the time when he was engaged in directing the
works of the Rhone and Saone at Lyons, as he mentions in his *Memoirs*, he wrote a treatise on the

construction of mills. He wished that D'Alembert should read it, to verify the mathematical calculations, and for this purpose he had put it into the hands of Morellet. D'Alembert approved of the essay ; and my father became advantageously known to Morellet as a man of science, and as one who had gratuitously and honourably conducted a useful work in France. His predominating taste thus continued, as in former times, its influence, was still a connecting link between him and old and new friends. On this and many other occasions he proved the truth of what has been asserted, that no effort is ever lost : his exertions at Lyons in 1772, after an interval of thirty years, now becoming of unexpected advantage to him and to his family at Paris. . . .

'In Paris there is an institution resembling our London Society of Arts, *La Société d'Encourage-ment pour l'Industrie Nationale* : of this my father was made a member, and he presented to it the model of a lock of his invention. In getting this executed, he became acquainted with some of the working mechanics in Paris, and had an opportunity of observing how differently work of this kind is carried on there and in Birmingham. Instead of the assemblage of artificers in manufactories, such as we see in Birmingham, each artisan in Paris, working out his own purposes in his own domicile, must in his

time " play many parts," and among these many to
which he is incompetent, either from want of skill or
want of practice: so that, in fact, even supposing
French artisans to be of equal ability and industry
with English competitors, they are at least a century
behind, by thus being precluded from all the
miraculous advantages of the division of labour. . . .

' My father had left England with a strong desire to
see Buonaparte, and had procured a letter from the
Lord Chamberlain (Lord Essex), and had applied to
Lord Whitworth, our Ambassador at Paris, who was
to present him.   But soon after our arrival at Paris,
he learned that Buonaparte was preparing the way
for becoming Emperor, contrary to the wishes and
judgment of the most enlightened part of the French
nation. . . .

' My father could no longer consider Buonaparte as
a great man, abiding by his principles, and content
with the true glory of being the first citizen of a free
people ; but as one meditating usurpation, and on the
point of overturning, for the selfish love of dominion,
the liberty of France.   With this impression, my
father declared that he would not go to the court of
a usurper.   He never went to his levées, nor would
he be presented to him.

' My father had not the presumption to imagine that
in a cursory view, during a slight tour, and a residence

of four or five months at Paris, he could become thoroughly acquainted with France. Besides, his living chiefly with the select society which I have described precluded the possibility of seeing much of what were called *les nouveaux riches*.

'The few general observations he made on French society at this time I shall mention. He observed that, among the families of the old nobility, domestic happiness and virtue had much increased since the Revolution, in consequence of the marriages which, after they lost their wealth and rank, had been formed, not according to the usual fashion of old French alliances, but from disinterested motives, from the perception of the real suitability of tempers and characters. The women of this class in general, withdrawn from politics and political intrigue, were more domestic and amiable. . . .

'With regard to literature he observed that it had considerably degenerated. For the good taste, wit, and polished style which had characterised French literature before the Revolution there was no longer any demand, and but few competent judges remained. The talents of the nation had been forced by circumstances into different directions. At one time, the hurry and necessity of the passing moment had produced political pamphlets and slight works of amusement, formed to catch the public revolutionary taste.

At another period, the contending parties, and the real want of freedom in the country, had repressed literary efforts. Science, which flourished independently of politics, and which was often useful and essential to the rulers, had meanwhile been encouraged, and had prospered. The discoveries and inventions of men of science showed that the same positive quantity of talent existed in France as in former times, though appearing in a new form.'

The charms of Paris and its society were rudely broken by Edgeworth receiving one morning a visit from a police officer requiring him immediately to attend at the Palais de Justice. Edgeworth was in bed with a cold when this summons came. He writes to Miss Charlotte Sneyd :—' My being ill was not a sufficient excuse ; I got up and dressed myself *slowly*, to gain time for thinking—drank one dish of choco-late, ordered my carriage, and went with my *exempt* to the Palais de Justice. There I was shown into a parlour, or rather a guard-room, where a man like an under-officer was sitting at a desk. In a few minutes I was desired to walk upstairs into a long narrow room, in different parts of which ten or twelve clerks were sitting at different tables. To one of these I was directed—he asked my name, wrote it on a printed card, and demanding half a crown, presented the card to me, telling me it was a passport. I told

him I did not want a passport ; but he pressed it upon me, assuring me that I had urgent necessity for it,
as I must quit Paris immediately. Then he pointed
out to me another table, where another clerk was
pleased to place me in the most advantageous point
of view for taking my portrait, and he took my written
portrait with great solemnity, and this he copied into
my passport. I begged to know who was the principal person in the room, and to him I applied to
learn the cause of the whole proceeding. He coolly
answered that if I wanted to know I must apply to
the *Grand Juge*. To the *Grand Juge* I drove, and
having waited till the number ninety-three was called,
the number of the ticket which had been given to me
at the door, I was admitted, and the *Grand Juge* most
formally assured me that he knew nothing of the
affair, *but* that all I had to do was to obey. I returned home, and, on examining my passport, found
that I was ordered to quit Paris in twenty-four hours.
I went directly to our Ambassador, Lord Whitworth,
who lived at the extremity of the town : he was ill—
with difficulty I got at his secretary, Mr. Talbot, to
whom I pointed out that I applied to my Ambassador
from a sense of duty and politeness, before I would
make any application to private friends, though I believed that I had many in Paris who were willing
and able to assist me. The secretary went to the

Ambassador, and in half an hour wrote an official note to Talleyrand, to ask the why and the wherefore. He advised me in the meantime to quit Paris, and to go to some village near it — Passy or Versailles. Passy seemed preferable, because it is the nearest to Paris—only a mile and a half distant. Before I quitted Paris I made another attempt to obtain some explanation from the *Grand Juge*. I could not see him, or even his secretary, for a considerable time ; and when at length the secretary appeared, it was only to tell me that I could not see the *Grand Juge*. " Cannot I write," said I, " to your *Grand Juge* ? " He answered hesitatingly, " Yes." A huissier took in my note, and another excellent one from the friend who was with me, F. D. The huissier returned presently, holding my papers out to me at arm's length—" The *Grand Juge* knows nothing of this matter."

' I returned home, dined, ordered a carriage to be ready to take me to Passy, wrote a letter to Buonaparte, stating my entire ignorance of the cause of my *déportation*, and asserting that I was unconnected with any political party. F. D. engaged that the letter should be delivered ; and Mrs. E. and Charlotte remaining to settle our affairs at Paris, I set off for Passy with Maria, where my friend F. D. had taken the best lodging he could find for me in the village. Madame G. had offered me her country house at

Passy; but though she pressed that offer most kindly
we would not accept of it, lest we should compromise
our friends. Another friend, Mons. de P., offered his
country house, but, for the same reason, this offer was
declined. We arrived at Passy about ten o'clock at
night, and though a *déporté*, I slept tolerably well.
Before I was up, my friend Mons. de P. was with me
—breakfasted with us in our little oven of a parlour
—conversed two hours most agreeably. Our other
friend, F. D., came also before we had breakfasted,
and just as I had mounted on a table to paste some
paper over certain deficiencies in the window, enter
M. P.—and Le B——h.

'"*Mon ami, ce n'est pas la peine !*" cried they both
at once, their faces *rayonnant de joie.* "You need not
give yourself so much trouble ; you will not stay here
long. We have seen the *Grand Juge,* and your detention arises from a mistake. It was supposed that
you are brother to the Abbé Edgeworth—we are to
deliver a petition from you, stating what your relation-
ship to the Abbé really is. This shall be backed by
an address signed by all your friends at Paris, and
you will be then at liberty to return."

'I objected to writing any petition, and at all events
I determined to consult my Ambassador, who had
conducted himself well towards me. I wrote to Lord
Whitworth, stating the facts, and declaring that

K

nothing could ever make me deny the honour of being related to the Abbé Edgeworth. Lord Whitworth advised me, however, to state the fact that I was not the Abbé's brother. . . .

' No direct answer was received from the First Consul ; but perhaps the revocation of the order of the *Grand Juge* came from him. We were assured that my father's letter had been read by him, and that he declared he knew nothing of the affair ; and so far from objecting to any man for being related to the Abbé Edgeworth, he declared that he considered him as a most respectable, faithful subject, and that he wished that he had many such.'

Before this unpleasant occurrence Edgeworth had thought of taking a house in Paris for two years and sending for his other children ; but he now, in spite of the entreaties of his French friends, altered his plans and resolved to return home. Maria writes :—' He was prudent and decided—had he been otherwise, we might all have been among the number of our countrymen who were, contrary to the law of nations, and to justice and reason, made prisoners in France at the breaking out of the war. We were fortunate in getting safe to free and happy England a short time before war was declared, and before the detention of the English took place.

' My eldest brother had the misfortune to be among

those who were detained. His exile was rendered as tolerable as circumstances would permit by the inde-fatigable kindness of our friends the D'——s. But it was an exile of eleven years—from 1803 to 1814—six years of that time spent at Verdun ! '

CHAPTER XI

INSTEAD of returning at once to Ireland, the Edge-
worths went to Edinburgh to visit Henry Edgeworth,
whose declining health caused his father much anxiety.
Maria writes :—' He mended rapidly while we were at
Edinburgh; and this improvement in his health added
to the pleasure his father felt in seeing the interest
his son had excited among the friends he had made
for himself in Edinburgh—men of the first abilities
and highest characters, both in literature and science
—whom we knew by their works, as did all the world ;
with some of whom my father had had the honour of
corresponding, but to whom he was personally unknown. Imagine the pleasure he felt at being introduced to them by his son, and in hearing Gregory,
Alison, Playfair, Dugald Stewart, speak of Henry as
if he actually belonged to themselves, and with the
most affectionate regard. . . .

'On our journey homewards, in passing through
Scotland, we met with much hospitality and kindness,
and much that was interesting in the country and in

its inhabitants. But the circumstance that remains the most fixed in my recollection, and that which afterwards influenced my father's life the most, happened to be the books we read during our last day's journey. These were the lives of Robertson the historian, and of Reid, which had been just given to us by Mr. Stewart. In the life of Reid there are some passages which struck my father particularly. I recollect at the moment when I was reading to him, his stretching eagerly across from his side of the carriage to mine, and marking the book with his pencil with strong and reiterated marks of approbation. The passages relate to the means which Dr. Reid employed to prevent the decay of his faculties as he advanced in years; to remedy the errors and deficiencies of one failing sense by the increased activity of another; and by the resources of reasoning and ingenuity to resist, as far as possible, or to render supportable, the infirmities of age. . . . My father never forgot this passage, and acted on it years afterwards.'

It was not Henry who was taken first, but Charlotte, who was 'fresh as a rose' on her first tour abroad. In April 1807 she died of the same disease as her sisters, and about two years after her brother Henry followed her to the grave.

It needed a brave heart to bear up under such sorrows, but Edgeworth, though he felt them keenly, would not sink into the lethargy of grief, but roused himself to work for the public good. He was on the board appointed to inquire into the education of the people of Ireland, and two of his papers on the subject were printed in the reports of the Commissioners; he also drew up the plan of a school for Edgeworth Town, which was afterwards carried into execution by his son, Lovell; and at this time he was writing his *Memoirs*, a task which was interrupted by a severe illness in 1809. He had hardly recovered from this before he was engaged in the Government survey of bogs, and Maria writes :—' It was late in the year, and the weather unfavourable. In laying out and verifying the work of the surveyors employed, he was usually out from daybreak to sunset, often fifteen hours without food, traversing on foot, with great bodily exertion, wastes and deserts of bog, so wet and dangerous as to be scarcely passable at that season, even by the common Irish best used to them. In these bogs there frequently occur great holes, filled with water of the same colour as the bog, or sometimes covered over with a slight surface of the peat heath or grass, called by the common people *a shaking scraw*.

' In traversing these bogs a man must pick his way carefully, sometimes wading, sometimes leaping from one landing place to another, choosing these cautiously, lest they should not sustain his weight: avoiding certain treacherous green spots on which the unwary might be tempted to set foot, and would sink, never to rise again.'

The work was fatiguing, but the open air life seemed to give him new vigour, and his health was re-established.

The work had interested him much, and he believed that an immense tract of bog might be reclaimed. The obstacles he foresaw were want of capital and the danger of litigation. As long as the bogs were unprofitable there was no incitement to a strict definition of boundaries, but if the land was reclaimed many lawsuits would follow. Maria thus describes the difficulties encountered by her father:—'He wished to undertake the improvement of a large tract of bog in his neighbourhood, and for this purpose desired to purchase it from the proprietor; but the proprietor had not the power or the inclination to sell it. My father, anxious to try a decisive experiment on a large scale, proposed to rent it from him, and offered a rent, till then unheard of, for bogland. The proprietor professed himself satisfied to accept the proposal, provided my father would undertake to indemnify him for any expense to which he might be put by future lawsuits concerning the property or boundaries of this bog. He was aware that if he were to give a lease for a long term, even for sixty years, this would raise the idea that the bog would become profitable ; and still further, if ever it should be really improved and profitable, it would become an object of contention and litigation to many who might fancy they had claims, which, as long as the bog was nearly without value, they found it not worth while to urge. It was impossible to enter into the *insurance* proposed, and, consequently, he could not obtain this tract of bog, or further prosecute his plan. The same sort of difficulty must frequently recur. Parts of different estates pass through extensive tracts of bog, of which the boundaries are uncertain. The right to cut the turf is usually vested in the occupiers of adjoining farms ; but they are at constant war with each other about boundaries, and these disputes, involving the original grants of the lands, hundreds of years ago, with all subsequent deeds and settlements, appear absolutely interminable. . . .

'It may not be at present a question of much interest to the British public, because no such large decisive experiment as was proposed has yet been tried as to the value and attainableness of the object ; but its magnitude and importance are incontestable, the whole extent of peat soil in Ireland exceeding, as it is confidently pronounced, 2,830,000 acres, of which about half might be converted to the general purposes of agriculture.'

It was in 1811 that Edgeworth constructed, 'upon a plan of his own invention, a spire for the church of Edgeworth Town. This spire was formed of a skeleton of iron, covered with slates, painted and sanded to resemble Portland stone. It was put together on the ground within the tower of the church, and when finished it was drawn up at once, with the assistance of counterbalancing weights, to the top of the tower, and there to be fixed in its place.

' The novelty of the construction of this spire, even in this its first skeleton state, excited attention, and as it drew towards its completion, and near the moment when, with its covering of slates, altogether amounting to many tons weight, it was to move, or not to move, fifty feet from the ground to the top of the tower, everybody in the neighbourhood, forming different opinions of the probability of its success or failure, became interested in the event.

' Several of my father's friends and acquaintances, in our own and from adjoining counties, came to see it drawn up. Fortunately, it happened to be a very fine autumn day, and the groups of spectators of different ranks and ages, assembled and waiting in silent expectation, gave a picturesque effect to the whole. A bugle sounded as the signal for ascent. The top of the spire appearing through the tower of the church, began to move upwards ; its gilt ball and arrow glittered in the sun, while with motion that was scarcely perceptible it rose majestically. Not one word or interjection was uttered by any of the men who worked the windlasses at the top of the tower.

'It reached its destined station in eighteen minutes, and then a flag streamed from its summit and gave notice that all was safe. Not the slightest accident or difficulty occurred.' Maria adds :—'The conduct of the whole had been trusted to my brother William (the civil engineer), and the first words my father said, when he was congratulated upon the success of the work, were that his son's steadiness in conducting business and commanding men gave him infinitely more satisfaction than he could feel from the success of any invention of his own.'

Towards the close of 1811 Edgeworth was requested, as he understood, by a committee of the House of Commons on *Broad Wheels*, to look over and report on a mass of evidence on the subject. This he did, but then found that it was a private request of the chairman, Sir John Sinclair, who begged that the report might be given to the Board of Agriculture. This Edgeworth declined, but wrote instead and pre- sented *An Essay on Springs applied to Carts* ; and in 1813 he published an essay on *Roads, and Wheel Carriages.* His daughter writes :—'In the course of the drudgery which he went through he received a great counterbalancing pleasure from the following passage, which he chanced to meet with in a letter to the committee, written by a gentleman to whom he was personally a stranger :—

'" Mr. Edgeworth was the first who pointed out the great benefit of springs in aiding the draught of horses. The subject deserves more attention than it has hitherto met with. No discovery relative to carriages has been made in our time of equal importance ; and the ingenious author of it deserves highly of some mark of public gratitude." '

Maria adds :—' Those ingenious ideas, which had been but the amusement of youth, as he advanced in life, he turned to public utility : for instance, the mode of conveying secret and swift intelligence, which he had suggested at first only to decide a trifling wager between him and some young nobleman, he afterwards improved into a national telegraph, and through all difficulties and disappointments persevered till it was established. In the same manner, his juvenile amusements with the sailing chariot led to experiments on the resistance of the air, which in more mature years he pursued in the patient spirit of philosophical investigation, and turned to good account for the real business of life, and for the advancement of science.

' On this subject, in the year 1783, he published in

the *Transactions of the Royal Society* (vol. 73) " An Essay on the Resistance of the Air," of which the object, as he states, is to determine the force of the wind upon surfaces of different size and figure, or upon the same surface, when placed in different directions, inclined at different angles, or curved in different arches. . . . After trying several experiments on surfaces of various shapes, he ascertained the difference of resistance in different cases, suggested the probable cause of these variations, and opened a large field for future curious and useful speculation ; *useful* it may be called, as well as curious, because such knowledge applies immediately to the wants and active business of life, to the construction of wind- and water-mills, and to the extensive purposes of navigation. The theory of philosophers and the practice of mechanics and seamen were, and perhaps are still, at variance as to the manner in which sails of wind-mills and of ships should be set. Dr. Hooke, in his day, expressed " his surprise at the obstinacy of seamen in continuing, after what appeared the clearest demonstration to the contrary, to prefer what are called bellying or bunting sails, to such as are hauled tight." The doctor said that he would, at some future time, add the test of experiment to mathematical investigation in support of the theory.

'It is remarkable that this test of experiment, when at length it was applied, confirmed the truth of what the philosopher had reprobated as an obstinate vulgar error. My father, in his *Essay on the Resistance of the Air*, gives the result of his experiments on a flat and curved surface of the same dimensions, and explains the cause of the error into which Dr. Hooke, M. Parent, and other mathematicians had fallen in their theoretic reasonings. . . .

'It is remarkable that a man of naturally lively imagination and of inventive genius should not, in science, have ever followed any fanciful theory of his own, but that all he did should have been characterised by patient investigation and prudent experiment. . . .

'In science, it is not given to man *to finish*; to persevere, to advance a step or two, is all that can be accomplished, and all that will be expected by the real philosopher.

'" *We will endeavour*," is the humble and becoming motto of our philosophical society.'

In his seventy-first year Edgeworth had a dangerous illness, and though he seemed to recover from it for a time, he never regained his former strength. One great privation was that, from the failure of his sight, he became dependent on others to read and write for him. But his cheerful fortitude did not fail, though he felt that his days were numbered. He had promised to try some private experiments for the Dublin Society, and with the help of his son William he carried out a set of experiments on wheel carriages in April 1815 and in May 1816.

Almost his last literary effort was to dictate some pages which he contributed to his daughter Maria's novel *Ormond*, and he delighted in having the proof-sheets read to him and in correcting them. Mrs. Ritchie has given some touching details of his last days in her Introduction to a new edition of *Ormond*.

Maria writes :—'The whole of Moriaty's history, and his escape from prison, were dictated without any alteration, or hesitation of a word, to Honora and me. This history Mr. Edgeworth heard from the actual hero of it, Michael Dunne, whom he chanced to meet in the town of Navan, where he was living respectably. He kept a shop where Mr. Edgeworth went to purchase some boards, and observing something very remarkable about the man's countenance, he questioned him as they were looking at the lumber in his yard, and Dunne readily told his tale almost in the very words used by Moriaty. . . . Mr. Edgeworth also wrote the meeting between Moriaty and his wife when he jumps out of the carriage the moment he hears her voice.'

Edgeworth kept his intellectual faculties to the last. ' To the last they continued clear, vigorous, energetic ; and to the last were exerted in doing good, and in fulfilling every duty, public and private. . . .

' In the closing hours of his life his bodily sufferings subsided, and in the most serene and happy state, he said, before he sank to that sleep from which he never wakened :—

'" I die with the soft feeling of gratitude to my friends and submission to the God who made me." '

He died the 13th of June 1817.

It may be thought to be an easy task to make an abridgment of a biography, but in some ways it is almost as difficult as it is for the sketcher to choose what he will put into his picture and yet preserve a due proportion and give a faithful idea of the whole scene before him.   I have tried to give such portions of the *Memoirs* as will present the many-sided character of R. L. Edgeworth in relation to his scientific, literary, and educational work, and in relation to his position as a landlord, a father, and a friend.   He was a singular instance of great mental activity with little ambition ; of a genial nature in his own family circle and among his friends, he withdrew from the multitude, and refused to lower his standard of cultivated intercourse in order to win favour with coarser natures.   He is chiefly remembered now as an educational reformer and as the guide of Maria Edgeworth in the earlier stages of her literary career. What she achieved was in great part due to her father's judicious training and encouragement.

A little more ambition and the spur of poverty might have made Edgeworth better known as an inventor of useful machines : it is curious to remark how nearly he invented the bicycle.   He saw the advantage that light railways would be to Ireland, but the breath of mechanical life, steam, as a power, he did not foresee.

He might have written a book on 'The Domestic Life,' so fully had he mastered the secrets of a happy home. He was naturally passionate, but had trained himself to be on his guard against his temper, and was always anxious to improve and to correct any bad habit or fault : even in old age he was constantly on the watch lest bodily infirmities should lead to moral deterioration. He was not too proud to own when he had made mistakes, but used the experience he had gained, and carefully studied his own character and the circumstances which had been most beneficial in forming it. He controlled his expenses as prudently as his temper, and would not allow his inventive faculties to lead him into unjustifiable outlays. His daughter mentions that 'when he was a youth of nineteen, an old gentleman, who saw him passing by his window, said of him, judging by the liveliness of his manner and appearance, " There goes a young fellow who will in a few years dissipate all the fortune his prudent father has been nursing for him his whole life."

'The prophecy was, by a kind neighbour, repeated to him, and, as I have heard him say, it made such an impression as tended considerably to prevent its own accomplishment.

' He acquired the habit of calculating and forming estimates most accurately. He not only estimated what every object of fancy and taste would cost, but he accustomed himself to consider what the actual enjoyment of the indulgence would be. . . . He upon all occasions carefully separated the idea of the pleasure of possession from that of contemplating any object of taste.'

She also mentions that 'he observed, that the happiness that people derive from the cultivation of their understandings is not in proportion to the talents and capacities of the individual, but is compounded of the united measure of these, and of the use made of them by the possessor ; this must include good or ill temper, and other moral dispositions. Some with transcendent talents waste these in futile projects ; others make them a source of misery, by indulging that overweening anxiety for fame which ends in disappointment, and excites too often the powerful passions of envy and jealousy ; others, too humble, or too weak, fret away their spirits and their life in deploring that they were not born with more abilities. But though so many lament the want of talents, few actually derive as much happiness as they might from the share of understanding which they possess. My father never wasted his time in deploring the want of that which he could by exertion acquire. Nor did he suffer fame in any pursuit to be his first object.'

We feel that we are in the moral atmosphere of Paley and Butler when she adds :—'Far beyond the pleasures of celebrity, or praise in any form, he classed self-approbation and benevolence : these he thought the most secure sources of satisfaction in this world.' This is the spirit of the Eighteenth Century, the clear cold tone of the moral philosopher, not the enthusiastic impulse of the fervid theologian, of Pusey, Keble, or Newman. One star does indeed differ from another in glory, but all give brilliance to our firmament and raise our thoughts from earth.

Such a life as Richard Edgeworth's seems to me to be more instructive than even that excellent moral guide-book written by Sir John Lubbock, *The Uses of Life*, because abstract maxims take less hold of uncultivated or unanalytical minds than the portrait of a man of flesh and blood. Bunyan's *Pilgrim's Progress* reaches many hearts which are unmoved by an ordinary sermon, and Edgeworth's life was indeed a *progress*, a constant striving not only to improve himself but to help others onward in the right way. He showed what a good landlord could do in Ireland, and what a good father can do in binding a family in happy union.

www.ingramcontent.com/pod-product-compliance
Lightning Source LLC
Chambersburg PA
CBHW030900050726
47500CB00009B/550